The Guild's Demands

Book 7 of the
Adventures on Brad

By

Tao Wong

Copyright

This is a work of fiction. Names, characters, businesses, places, events and incidents are either the products of the author's imagination or used in a fictitious manner. Any resemblance to actual persons, living or dead, or actual events is purely coincidental.

This book is licensed for your personal enjoyment only. This book may not be re-sold or given away to other people. If you would like to share this book with another person, please purchase an additional copy for each recipient. If you're reading this book and did not purchase it, or it was not purchased for your use only, then please return to your favorite book retailer and purchase your own copy. Thank you for respecting the hard work of this author.

A Starlit Publishing Book
Published by Starlit Publishing
PO Box 30035, High Park PO
Toronto, ON
M6P 3K0
Canada

www.starlitpublishing.com

Ebook ISBN: 9781989994894
Paperback ISBN: 9781989994900

Contents

Chapter 1

"Daniel Chai?"

The voice caught the adventurer as he wandered down from the stairs, running a hand through still-wet brown hair. The wooden railings of the worn medieval inn pressed on his hands, the wood helping to guide him down after a late night of revelry. A smile still lingered on Daniel's lips as he recalled the young lady he'd left behind in his bed, asleep after a night of vigorous exercise. He only wished he could remember her name.

The broad-shouldered adventurer turned his head, spotting the speaker seated at his table and positioned to catch sight of those descending from the inn's second floor. He raised the battered wooden mug, filled with weak ale in greeting to Daniel.

"Will you join me?"

Daniel frowned, a hand dropping down to his side where his enchanted mace hung. He had put on the mace automatically, even though he was still dressed in his civilian tunic and pants which needed patching by the laundress after his most recent escapade in the dungeons of Silverstone. He kept meaning to pick up a few more pairs, but there was always something better to do.

"Do I know you?" Daniel asked.

"No, but I hope to change that with this breakfast," the stranger said.

Peering closer, Daniel took note of the finer weave of his clothes, the lack of fraying along the edges, the pair of rings with runic inscriptions on them, and the top of the bejewelled dagger that poked above the table from the stranger's belt. It all spoke of an individual with funds to burn, entirely unlike Daniel himself and his friends.

It wasn't as though they were hurting for money these days. As Advanced Adventurers, Daniel and his team earned decent coin delving the dungeons on the regular. But having lost both new members of their impromptu party, the remaining trio were under-strength for dungeons that consisted of the city of Silverstone. Attempts at finding new party members had, thus far, been less than successful, as most independent adventurers of quality sought to join the various guilds that made up the city.

Of course, it left the trio to work the first few levels of each of the dungeons over and over again. In truth, the repetition was relaxing, as they quietly and steadily saved up for more powerful, enchanted equipment to allow them to delve deeper.

Daniel hesitated for a second before deciding to accept the invitation. While unusual, it was possible that the stranger was a client, someone seeking adventurers too cheap to use the official Adventurer's Guild board.

As Daniel took a seat, he did have to point out: "I have paid for my breakfast already. It comes with the room."

"Yes, I know." The stranger grinned, pearlescent white teeth flashing, underneath sky-blue eyes. The shock of pale, yellow hair, almost transparent in its coloring and fineness, flopped in an artful wave across the stranger's face. "Which is why I paid for your accommodation." Daniel's eyes widened a little, since the night's accommodation was significantly more expensive than a single meal. It widened further as the stranger continued. "For the week."

"You must really want to talk," Daniel said.

"I do." Before the stranger could continue, he was interrupted by the innkeeper who tromped out of the kitchen carrying a trencher of sausages, eggs, and blood pudding. He slapped the trencher down before Daniel, before turning away and stomping back into his kitchen. The stranger's eyes crinkled with humor as Daniel shrugged and withdrew his belt knife.

"You don't mind, do you?"

"Not at all. After all, I did pay for it," the man said, reminding Daniel not at all subtly.

Ravenously, Daniel speared the sausage, slicing it up and popping it into his mouth, chewing upon it and enjoying the taste sweeping through his mouth. The innkeeper of the Burnt Table might be lacking in his early-morning graces but more than made up for it with his cooking ability. It was the primary reason Daniel stayed at this location, together with the deal he received from the innkeeper for helping with his injured foot. Even Daniel's Gift, able to fix numerous issues with the physical body, could not heal the curse that the man was under. He could only relieve the pain the ex-adventurer felt on a regular basis.

"Before we go any further, I should introduce myself. I am Mattias Gill of the Three Skills Guild," Mattias said. He paused, lifting expectant eyes to Daniel.

He was not disappointed. Daniel stopped chewing for a few moments, before continuing to pop chunks of blood sausage into his mouth. The kitchen door swung open again, bringing the innkeeper with his mug of water. As he set the drink down, Mattias gestured for another mug almost immediately. The innkeeper snorted but tromped back to the bar to pour another mug of ale. This late in the morning, it was no surprise there were no other guests in the inn. Those who stayed at the inn were generally adventurers like Daniel, and most would have left early to seek new quests or begin a delve.

It was only because Daniel and his team had come back yesterday from a multi-day exploration outside the city, completing a well-paying—but long—process of overseeing the planting of crops, that he was even here. Today was a rest day, and Daniel had plans to visit the local hospices on his usual rounds.

Somehow, he did not think that his plans were going to play out today.

"And what would the Three Skills Guild want with me?" Daniel asked. The guild was one of the larger, most powerful associations in the kingdom of Brad, though its power mainly came from the numerous nobles and their connections. Rumors abounded that they had close connections, maybe even a hold, on the current royalty. Most of those rumors also tied them to certain unsavory acts, though most of those were just that—rumors. They also had a few well-provisioned and well-equipped delving teams, but for the most part, it was just rich crafters. Crafting, running merchant stalls, and providing information services were what the Three Skills Guild were best known for.

Their name was a bit of a misnomer, for the Guild had pivoted in its origins from a mercenary guild to its current status over a hundred and fifty years ago. Many of the original members had acquired their noble lineage, giving them the strong connections they were rumored for. Still, the Guild kept its name for the sake of tradition.

"Oh, simply with an offer," said Mattias. "We are desperate to build up proper adventuring teams, and you and yours fit the bill."

Daniel raised an eyebrow skeptically. "That's nice to hear, if a little improbable. We did well at the contests, but not that well."

"Well, the Guild is pivoting its direction slightly and will be looking for more advanced junior Adventurers, other than cherry picking from the top," Mattias said.

As hard as Daniel scrutinized the man, he could not find the lie. However, he knew that what Mattias spoke of was, at best, stretching the truth. There was no way that the Three Skills was looking so far down the ladder to pick up new Advanced Adventurers like them. Maybe in a couple of years, once they cleared at least one advanced dungeon.

Of course, Daniel was also skeptical, for he'd already turned down quite a few other invitations. All of them, at least in the more recent groups, had couched it in terms that did not focus upon his value to them as an Adventurer but as a healer.

Healers continued to be a large deficit in the adventuring economy, with few individuals having either the skills or the spells to fill that role. While powerful, potions were limited in use due to both their relative rarity and potential toxicity. That left healers to cover the gap. However, traditional healers only advanced from the process of healing, the usage of their skills. Traveling into a dungeon was not only damaging to their overall progress, it was dangerous.

"Well, thank you for the offer," Daniel said. He gestured with one grease-stained hand pointing up toward the roof and added, "As well as the room."

"You haven't even heard my offer yet," Mattias said.

"I know. But I've heard a lot of others," Daniel said. "I don't see how it'd be that different."

"Oh, but ours is," Mattias said. He dropped his voice as he leaned in to whisper, "We will help keep your secret safe."

"Secret?"

"About your Gift."

The blood drained from Daniel's face, giving the game away. Not that it mattered, for Mattias looked very confident that the information he had uttered was entirely accurate. Daniel's secret, his most closely guarded secret, had finally been disclosed—and likely, all his dreams with them.

***

Of course, Daniel tried to prevaricate and downplay his reaction, but Mattias just smiled, until Daniel sighed and, glancing around the empty inn, spoke. "What do you know?"

"That you have a Gift for healing, which is not related to your Mana, and its abilities seem to reach levels of at least a Master Healer," Mattias said, leaning back and smiling. "There are some issues with the Gift—the Price, obviously—though my spies have not been able to ascertain what Price that is." He inclined his head to Daniel. "Well done on that, by the way. All too often, the Gifted let that slip. In most cases, it matters not. In some cases, it has mattered greatly."

Daniel nodded. The stories were clear on that. The fall of the Hero Sasno when he was betrayed and his wealth taken was legend. Another was the tragedy of Sylvia when she was forced to sacrifice her sense of feeling, again and again for the amusement of the nobles who desired the beauty that her gift crafted for them. Their world was replete with such tales, and Daniel was certain the Beastkin and others had their own stories.

Even the rise of the Orc Champion Hoze Manslayer was tied to his twisted Gift. How he was forced to sacrifice his own family for the strength he gained, twisting the original Gift he had been given because of his dealings with Ba'al. Though . . . Daniel sometimes wondered if that version, the common version, was but a perversion of the truth. Propaganda. Though, it might not be intentional—there was much bad blood between the Orc Tribes and the human kingdoms.

"It matters," Daniel said, finally. That much, he felt, was suitable to offer. "But, if you learned it, won't others? And a threat . . ."

"Not a threat. An offer," Mattias said immediately. "You don't threaten healers. Not if you're smart." He laughed softly. "Especially a skilled one. Could you imagine an angry healer refusing to heal you when you most need it? What a disaster."

Daniel could. And he could imagine how one could ensure compliance. People, humans, broke under enough pain. He had seen it in the hospice, in the clinics where he worked and watched former strong men and women crushed under the unrelenting pain of badly healed injuries, of diseases and sicknesses that had no normal cure. Faced with a lifetime of agony, they crumbled, willing to accept any outlet, any method of escape. Some chose the ultimate escape of death while others overused the few potions and drugs that could provide relief.

Magic could fix much, but it cost too much, was out of the grasp of too many. It was not possible to heal all those who needed it, and so mundane medicine had to make up the difference. And even then, the cost was often out of the reach of the lowest of the low.

It was, in truth, his own experiences in the mines, working with those in need, that kept Daniel going back. More than practice to further his own education, it was the need to help that drove him to the hospices on his days off from adventuring.

Which, he had to admit, was likely the reason why he was here, too, in this time and place, with his secret exposed. For all too often, he'd tapped into his Gift when he shouldn't have. When a case touched him and he secretly adjusted a body beyond what normal magic might make possible.

"No, what we offer is protection. Help. As you might realize, the Three Skills are not your typical guild," Mattias said, oblivious to Daniel's self-recrimination and thoughts. "We are, for want of a better term, connected. And that connection is what you need." Daniel frowned, but Mattias continued unperturbed. "We have spies and informants throughout the kingdom. It gives us a lead on interesting new Dungeons and quests. We would be able to head off rumors about you for a long time and, eventually, mitigate the demands on your time."

"Mitigate?" Daniel said.

"Reduce."

"Oh." Daniel nodded. "But not remove."

"It depends on the extent of your Gift, of course, but what little we know, it is unlikely." Mattias opened his hands wide. "The fact remains, healing continues to be a significant concern. And while the King and his family—long may they rule" —Daniel echoed the ritual proclamation by instinct— "are in good health, the need for a powerful healer is always there."

Daniel made a face but nodded. He looked at Mattias for a second, before he finally nodded. "Thank you. I need . . . time to think about it. And to speak with my party."

"Of course," Mattias said, smiling. He pushed his mug away, standing up. "Just ask at the Guild hall if you want to find us. We're quite well known." Mattias paused, waiting for Daniel to meet his gaze before he continued. "Just don't take too long."

Daniel nodded, watching the man walk out the door before he swigged on his own mug of ale. A short while later, a slender Catkin took a seat across from Daniel, her bare, padded feet never making a sound on the floorboards. Yet, somehow, in brief moments, a plate of stew and a drink appeared before the young lady, the innkeeper offering Asin a simple nod before leaving.

"Did you hear?" Daniel asked when they were alone.

Asin offered a curt nod, her cat-ears at the top of her head swiveling a little as they picked up additional noises from the street. Daniel well knew that her senses—sight, hearing, smell to a lesser extent—were all stronger than his own human ones. Stronger than most Beastkin even, for the Catkin was closer to her beast ancestors—more "pure" in her blood—than many that lived in Brad. It meant her body was covered with fur, her features more cat-like than many others who might pass as humans with barely any beast features. But it provided her certain other advantages too, like her extended senses, and disadvantages like her altered vocal box that made it hard to talk in human languages.

"QuanEr's tears," Daniel cursed softly. "I'm sorry. I knew I shouldn't have. . . . This . . . I . . ."

Asin snorted at Daniel, making him look over at the Catkin. She slowly and carefully spooned some of the stew into her mouth, chewing on the strips of meat before swallowing. "Expected. Worry later."

Daniel nodded, then glanced upwards. "Omrak awake yet?"

"Not here," Asin said.

"He's already left?"

Asin shook her head.

"He never came back?"

A nod.

"Oh." Daniel grinned. "Finally."

Asin nodded again. The pair shared conspiratorial smiles. For all Omrak's large and robust personality, he was also somewhat shy among young ladies, never having truly interacted with them. The past few months however had seen him thawing and beginning to savor the advantages of being an Advanced Adventurer.

Not to say that the Northerner was not keeping an eye out for a potential wife. As he often mentioned, he needed a strong and sturdy wife for when he eventually returned home and took up sheepherding and farming once again.

"Damn. I guess I'll tell him later. Tonight or tomorrow . . ." Daniel trailed off, uncertain of what else to do. Normally, he'd be leaving for the hospice by now. But with this news, he was uncertain if that was the right choice. In fact, it was possible he should . . .

"Asin?" He blinked, surprise in his voice as the Catkin stood up, waving goodbye to him. "Where are you going?"

The Catkin pointed to the doorway, making Daniel's jaw drop. While he tried to figure out a proper objection, Asin traipsed right out, leaving Daniel alone with his own concerns. He frowned, crossing his arms as he stared at the empty doorway.

"Well, fat lot of good you are," he said. "Now what am I supposed to do?" he whined, mostly to himself as he stared around the empty walls. For all the potential danger to his career, to his future, the threat was still in the future.

Chapter 2

Uncertain what to do, Daniel found himself making his way to the hospice. Even if his actions would increase the danger he was in, he could not really stop. For one thing, there was always work to be done. And for another, at this point, it was just a matter of time. He had no true illusions that if the Three Skills Guild could not get him, they would not sell what knowledge they had to another.

Which meant that the decision he had been putting off for so long was finally coming to a head. He needed to join a guild. Not a small guild either, but a substantial one like the Three Skills to gain their protection. It was only under their protection and the Adventurers Guild that he might be able to offset some of the incoming pressure from the royal family.

Even so, he expected that at some point, they'd still demand his services. But if he could negotiate that to be as needed rather than an on-call basis, he could still retain some freedom.

That would require support, which meant a large guild.

Luckily, his secondary skillset as a healer was well known. He actually had quite a few invitations. The question then was, who.

Mentally, Daniel went over his options as he checked into the hospice, said his greetings, washed his hands, and got ready to see the first of his patients.

Of course, at the top of any Adventurer's list was the Burning Fields Guild. They were the premiere guild in the kingdom. They were renowned for their exploits, the Dungeons they had cleared, the Quests they had completed, the levels their party members had gained. At the end of the day, they were the guild that everyone aspired to join.

Daniel even had a contact in one of their Advanced Class parties, the sister of the young boy he'd once saved. If he tried using her as a contact, perhaps he could join them. Their size and their reputation would serve him well with regard to the royal family and nobles. More so than any others.

But he hadn't really considered joining them for several reasons. Firstly, they didn't recruit in the guild house in Silverstone. While they often ran parties through Advanced Dungeons, unlike many other guilds, they did so on a rotational basis with the intent to introduce new members to as much variety as possible. Once a Dungeon was cleared, the party would move on to the next town, the next Dungeon. It was only in the capital with its numerous Advanced, Expert, and Master Class dungeons that manned recruiters were posted. They were large enough to do so, since those who truly were intent on joining would make their way over.

Secondly, he certainly hadn't intended to go to the capital. While it was much larger and there were more Adventurers, healers were still in short supply. Putting himself in that position would be like walking an unarmed villager in front of a goblin—never a smart idea.

And lastly, Daniel had to admit to himself, as a team, they were unexceptional. Better than normal perhaps, but that was in a medium-sized town like Silverstone. In the capital, he would be surprised if they were considered anything more than slightly better than average.

And even though a guild would probably take him, Daniel was uncertain if they would take his team. As the premier guild, they had more choice than most and while healers were always desirable, he had much less of a bargaining position with them.

Next up in terms of size were the Seven Stones Guild. Like the Red Roses or the Green Robin, it was a larger guild with locations in multiple cities and had the requisite backing and resources that signified and it was how they had, in their own way, pitched themselves to him. Of course, the others didn't have the same level of obtuseness like the Seven Stones vice-guildmaster Gadi, but they all provided the same kind of opportunity. Everything from a salary to discounted enchanted equipment and standard basic gear were all part of their recruitment package. Training and guidance were another major bonus when joining a large guild, though they also came with significant regulations and demands.

In contrast, there were smaller guilds like the Bent Nails or the Broken Chains, where Tevfik, Asin's ex-boyfriend, was allied. They were local guilds, large and powerful locally but unable to provide additional backing outside of their city. These smaller guilds would be Daniel's personal preference, since the increased autonomy suited his own personality.

But with the looming threat of noble and royal pressure, Daniel could not help but discard them. It was just not viable. A local city-sized guild could provide him few resources and would have little leeway when dealing with the royal family or even a powerful noble family.

"Are we done?" The hesitant voice brought Daniel back to his surroundings, to see a young mother shyly speaking to him. Daniel smiled, checked the bandage he'd been winding around the child's foot to ensure it was secure before he spoke. "Yes. Just make sure to keep the bandages clean and to wash with the boiled, herbal tincture. And don't forget to buy the herbs." He glared at the woman, knowing there was only a fifty-fifty chance she would. "And if it becomes red and inflamed, or if there is any pus, bring her back. Immediately. As long as she keeps the injury clean and washed, it should scab over and heal in a few weeks."

The mother nodded along to his repeated orders, offering Daniel another smile of thanks. He watched her take her daughter away, a part of him trying to remember exactly how the child had hurt herself. Running around somewhere, he vaguely recalled. It really didn't matter; the injury was painful but not life-threatening as long as it was cleaned and sewn shut.

"Next?" Daniel called out, moving to wash his hands again. Simple rituals of cleanliness and care were well-known, at least to healers and those who paid attention to the words of QuanEr. Goddess of mercy and redemption, of love and medicine, the goddess had spoken long of the needs of the sick while she worked to provide comfort.

The door to the small clinic room swung open, and a man shuffled in, arm clutched around his torso. Daniel's gaze swept over his new patient's form, taking in details of the man, the paleness in his face, the slight yellow color to his skin, the way he hunched over on his right. He sighed, gesturing for the man to take a seat.

"I'm going to take your hand now and send some healing energy into you. Just hold still," Daniel said. Suiting actions to word, Daniel tapped into his Gift with a brief flicker of will. It flowed through him, as natural as breathing or blinking, entering the patient's body. The answers came back quickly, the details washing away assumptions that Daniel had made. Not a lack of foodstuff or failing kidneys, but a parasite that had entered the body, eating away at his body and the organs.

He could fix it, but Daniel pulled away. As he did so, he felt something, a memory of playing with a rock lizard, slip away. Drifting off, leaving him with only portions. Of finding it and burying it when it had accidentally been hurt. But nothing of the time between. Once more, Daniel reeled, feeling a profound sense of loss—and yet, unable to really know what he had lost.

"Honored healer. Are you okay?" The man's voice was rough, worn from years of use. Concerned as Daniel swiped at his eyes.

"I'm fine," Daniel said, clearing his throat. "It's fine. You have a two-mouthed goplad parasite. Probably from some meat you ate recently. Visit the local herbalist and tell them that. They'll provide you with a poison-cleanse." As the man blanched, Daniel shook his head. "It's fine. You'll shit yourself a lot and maybe throw up a little. But if you take it for a few days, it'll clear out the parasites. The damage to your kidneys is permanent, unless you can come back in the next few days and a Minor Healing spell is cast."

"It's permanent?" the man said, wide-eyed. "Can't you . . . ?"

"Heal it now?" Daniel shook his head. "The parasites must be killed first. Take the medicine. Come back at the end of the day in five days when they're eradicated. If we have Mana to heal you, we'll cast the spell then. Even if we do, it won't fix it completely. In either case, you'll just have to accept the damage and find work that is less physically strenuous."

"But you're the miracle healer!" the man said, his eyes wide and insistent. "I came here because they say you can heal anything!"

"They're wrong," Daniel growled. "There's nothing more I can do for you."

It was a lie of course, but the damage was not life-threatening. And while it would be inconvenient for the man, Daniel was not about to use his Gift to fix a non-life-threatening injury.

"Yes, you can. They told me you could! I'm a Laborer! What am I supposed to do if I can't carry things?" the man said, raising his fist and waving it at Daniel. Daniel frowned, concern flashing through him. Lesser Strength was a common laborer skill, and depending on his Level, it might even be Greater Strength or one of its variants. A dangerous skill in close quarters. "No one needs a Laborer who's weak!"

Daniel leaned back, scooting his chair away as he lowered his voice to speak calmly. "I understand that's frustrating. But surely you have other skills? You can multi-class, can't you?"

"I'm Level 23! I'm too old to start gaining a new Class. And all my skills are strength and endurance-based. What do you think I could become? A Wagon Driver? A-a Shopkeeper? At my age?" He spat to the side. "I'm a Laborer. I'm good at it. Just heal me. You can do it!"

"I can't. Not with the parasites in you." Daniel stopped moving, now that he was out of easy punching range. He felt his heartbeat speed up a little at the potential threat, though the Laborer was much less of one than your typical Dungeon monster. Then again, Daniel was missing his usual equipment. "You have to kill them first."

"So you'll heal me, afterwards?" the Laborer said, leaning forwards and then sucking in a deep breath as his side pained him. Rage cooled a little, the surge of energy started to dim, reminding the Laborer of the pain he was in.

"Maybe."

The Laborer's face flushed with anger again, but Daniel had enough. He stood up, looming over the still-seated Laborer and leaned forwards, subtly flexing his muscles. As a former miner and now regular Adventurer, Daniel was no weak healer.

"I said maybe. There are many others who need healing. And those parasites—they only turn up in certain types of dungeon meats. Dungeon meats that a poor Laborer is unlikely to get, unless he was stealing it. Or getting it from the scraps at a higher-class restaurant," Daniel said. He watched as the last sentence made the Laborer flinch. "So what? You ate something that was thrown out and didn't even bother to cook it all the way through properly?"

"Me mate—Joey—said it was the way the nobs ate it. All bloody like."

"If it's fresh!" Daniel snapped. "Didn't you think there was a reason they threw it out?" Watching the Laborer flinch again, Daniel shook his head. "Just go. Take your herbs. And tell your mate to take the herbs too. The longer he waits, the more damage the parasites will do."

The Laborer stood up, hunched over, and shuffled out. Daniel sighed as he watched the man leave, turning over his words quietly. Miracle healer . . . it seemed he had been even less circumspect than he had thought. Then again, considering he'd only used his Gifts when even his magic was not sufficient, it made sense.

Before he could fall into further contemplation, a shout from the front office bearing his name had Daniel moving. Even without leaving his office, he knew what it was likely to be—another emergency requiring magical healing. Some industrial accident or a person run over, brought here to be fixed before they expired.

Dashing out, Daniel pushed further thoughts from his mind as he focused. Concerns about his future would have to wait while he saved some lives.

Chapter 3

"It seems, Friend Daniel, that we must make a decision soon," Omrak rumbled. The young, blond, and large Northerner replied after being informed of Daniel's morning encounter. He waved the haunch of shoulder around by its bone with one hand as he continued. "Perhaps it is a blessing in disguise."

Daniel raised an eyebrow. "Blessing?"

"Aye. We lack sufficient team members to truly explore the depths of the Dungeon. And while we grow stronger, we have yet to truly progress and will not without delving deeper."

By the large Adventurer's side, Asin offered a curt nod, a puffed piece of white bread filled with spiced meat slices in hand. Even from his seat on the opposite side of the table, Daniel's eyes watered a little from the smell of the spices in Asin's bread roll.

Swallowing around his salivating tongue, Daniel called up his own Status Screen to eye the changes he'd received since their last delve.

Name: Daniel Chai (Advanced Rank Adventurer)	Race: Human (Male)
Class: Level 14 Adventurer (14.2%)	Sub-classes: Level 6 (Miner) (87.6%)
Life: 360	Stamina: 360
Mana: 262	
Attributes	
Strength: 31	Agility: 25
Constitution: 34	Intelligence: 30
Willpower: 24	Luck: 17
Skills	
Unarmed Combat: Level 9 (03/100)	Clubs (Novice): Level 10 (17/100)
Archery: Level 3 (41/100)	Shield (Novice): Level 8 (71/100)
Dodge (Novice): Level 5 (37/100)	Combat Sense (Novice): Level 7 (86/100)
Perception (Novice): Level 4 (97/100)	Mining: Level 6 (34/100)

Healing (Novice): Level 7 (42/100)	Herb Lore: Level 4 (14/100)
Stealth: Level 2 (82/100)	Cooking: Level 4 (98/100)
Singing: Level 2 (11/100)	Tactics: Level 5 (55/100)
Heavy Armor : Level 2 (18/100)	
Skill Proficiencies	
Double Strike	Shield Bash
Perin's Blow	Find Weakness
Mapping (II)	Inventory (Adventurer Special)
Personal Armor (I)	
Spells	
Minor Healing (II)	Healer's Mark (I)
Gifts	
Martyr's Touch—The caster may heal oneself or others by touch and concentration, sacrificing a portion of his life to do so. Cost varies depending on the extent of the injuries healed.	

Upon their return and from their latest escort Quest, he had only managed to gain a single, miniscule Level. The issue for Daniel, sadly, was the loss of his Miner sub-class Level. Thankfully, he had not lost much in terms of his attributes—just a couple of points in Intelligence which he'd then replaced—when he lost his Level. His Gift might take some of his memory and knowledge when he breached an experience loss, but changes in his body were untouched. Mostly, it had affected how much Mana he was able to manage, which was frustrating.

With the new Skill Proficiency that he had gained, Daniel had dedicated the point towards his new heavy armor skill, picking up **Personal Armor**. It was a passive Skill Proficiency which made any armor he wore mold itself to his body as though it was customized for him. It was a subtle but powerful skill that gave him the full range of motion he was used to outside of armor while making the armor itself sit more centrally on his body and reduce pinching. That made it feel like significantly less weight, an important factor when one wore the armor for days at a time.

There were rumors that at higher levels of Skill Proficiency, the **Personal Armor** proficiency would even enchant armor—or reduce enchantment conflicts. Of course, those were the kinds of advancements an Expert Adventurer might have, individuals in the high-40s or even 50s of Levels.

"I guess you're right," Daniel finally said, closing his Status Screen with an exertion of will. "Which guild do you think we should join?"

"Mmm . . . Definitely not the Burning Fields," Omrak rumbled. Seeing Daniel's surprise, Omrak continued. "I have been speaking with other Adventurers, and many of those at the lowest rungs find the guild's resources dedicated towards the successful."

"Normal," Asin chuffed. Her tail lashed out behind her lazily as she took another bite of the meat bun.

"Not to the extent they speak of," Omrak said. "It seems that those who do not succeed gain very little resources."

"What do you mean by succeed?" Daniel said.

"Ah, that is interesting. Each Adventuring team is given a set series of objectives they must complete. Often a certain number of resources that they must bring in, a value in gold or levels cleared. If a team fails, the resources provided are reduced, with more successful teams given bonuses which are taken away from the resources given to others," Omrak said. "Each team competes with others in the same level."

"Do they use the color stages of the guild then for each level?" Daniel said. To further differentiate between Advanced Adventurers, each Adventurer was color coded. They were considered yellow adventurers, having graduated from the bottom of the barrel of reds.

"Yes. So we'd be competing with other yellow-ranked Adventurers." Omrak shook his head. "They say the competition is good for progress, but it forces their teams to focus almost exclusively on the Dungeons."

"I like Dungeons," Daniel pointed out. Quests, while fun and interesting, were often varied and significantly less financially rewarding than plain dungeon delving.

"Yes, but a man must have variety, Friend Daniel," Omrak replied. He looked over at Asin's meat bun before he continued. "Otherwise, everything tastes of the same three spices."

"Eleven," Asin said, incensed. She started growling in Beastkin, listing the spices out.

"Three or eleven, it's *hot!*" Omrak said.

"Weak."

"I am not weak," Omrak said, flexing his chest muscles. Asin snorted in amusement.

Rather than let his friends fall back into an old argument, Daniel spoke up. "Right. Not the Burning Fields, then. I like more control. Any you do like?"

"The Bent Nail?"

"No." Daniel shook his head. "Too small."

"Ah, but they can be quite persuasive," Omrak said.

"We know what kind of persuasion they used on you," Daniel drawled. The female-majority guild had often joined the team for dinner, trying to convince Daniel to join the smaller guild by parading a variety of young, interested female Adventurers before him.

"Hah! I noticed you and Emanuel were quite close for a while," Omrak said.

"Two weeks," Daniel said. "We went out for two weeks."

"Why did that fail?" Omrak said.

"We wanted different things," Daniel said, crossing his arms.

Asin emitted a low inquisitive purr.

"She wanted to quit in a few years, be a merchant. Have kids," Daniel muttered. "I wasn't interested."

"A heavy discussion, for such an early stage," Omrak said.

"It was after they came back from the fourteenth floor," Daniel replied.

The pair of Adventurers blinked and then nodded. Almost in unison, they recalled that night when the guild had stumbled in looking weary and injured. They had nearly lost half the team, and if not for the use of high-level healing potions, would have. As it was, the guild was now spending their time grinding the middle floors to earn enough income to purchase more potions of major healing.

"Ah. Yes. One does find oneself contemplating the frailness of one's mortal life after such encounters. Certainty of the future is often sought. As well as confirmation of one's survival," Omrak said.

"We did the last part for sure," Daniel said with a grin before he shrugged. "Anyway, they won't work. Any other suggestions?"

Omrak fell silent for a time, before he ticked his fingers off as he spoke, having placed the slab of meat down. "The Green Robin are perhaps most well known for the even-handedness of their actions. Though, they are also known for their lack of drive compared to the Burning Fields. Or so it's rumored. The Red Roses are well funded, well equipped, but have a high mortality rate. Their training is lacking, for all but their nobles. Still, many join for the connections and employment options after retirement."

"Isn't that true of any of the guilds? Like the Seven Stones?" Daniel said.

"That is true, but the nobles of the Red Roses hire their connections at a higher rate. It helps that they often run noble-exclusive Dungeons as well," Omrak said.

Daniel could only grunt at that. The existence of such Dungeons—sold off by the royal family at a premium—were a matter of contention among the commoners, the Adventurers, and nobles. Among commoners, the concern that a breakout might happen when a noble family declined from the positions of power to clear the Dungeon was always a concern. For Adventurers, blocking off entire Dungeons was aggravating, forcing them to compete with other Adventurers for resources and leveling spots. As for the nobles, the ability to acquire such Dungeons gave them a new and risky resource, one that could generate significant returns. Many a family had reversed their declines from the sudden appearance of a permanent or temporary Dungeon on their lands.

"I'm not that worried about retirement," Daniel said.

"I am," Omrak said.

"Yes," Asin added.

Daniel paused, looking between his friends before ducking his head in embarrassment. He forgot, sometimes, that not being healers, they did not have an easy fallback occupation. Especially when they would eventually retire as they grew older and slower, no longer able to take the risks as before. As he kept his head down, he grabbed his mug and sipped on the watered-down ale, tasting the hops within before he placed the drink down.

"Any others you'd suggest?" Daniel said.

"Well, there are a few larger guilds still. The White Scarves might not be as big but—"

"No," Asin said.

"Really?" Omrak said. "They have been one of the friendliest, if not the largest."

"To you," Asin said.

Daniel nodded slowly. He knew little of the White Scarves himself, though now that he thought of it, he could not remember a single Beastkin member among their parties. While antagonistic views about Beastkin had reduced over the years, there was still a strong anti-Kin element in Brad, driven by the Beastkin's different looks, their culture, and centuries-old conflict and enslavement. Even so, the Beastkin's stronger senses meant that most guilds would accept them into their parties as scouts and trap finders. Not every party, of course, but enough that you could find one or two Beastkin scattered throughout the guilds.

That, of course, raised the question of why Beastkin would even deign to enter guilds that might discriminate against them, but that was a matter of power imbalance. As Asin had explained, sometimes, you just took what you could. It wasn't as if they had much choice but to accept less-than-optimal deals.

"They're a problem?" Daniel said. Asin just nodded, and he shrugged, mentally marking them off. He'd look into it further, but it was true that they had never approached him either. Which left . . .

"The Beaten Steel," Omrak said. "Formed by the dwarf Willock Hammer. Though they've expanded to all the other races since their formation. They don't have much presence in Silverstone. I think there is that single party working the dungeons right now."

Daniel nodded. The guild mostly kept to the dungeons in the north, only sending parties out to other cities for the experience. They were highly insular, but had a large regional presence, thus allowing them to keep their presence as a second-tier large guild.

"Is that it?" Daniel said.

"Broken Chains." Asin said.

Daniel frowned. "Who?" A moment later, it struck him. "Isn't that the Beastkin guild?"

"Not just Kin," Asin said.

"Bah! The rest are rejects and outcasts." Omrak crossed his arms, shaking his head immediately. "They are not honorable company."

Asin's tail lashed out as she hissed and replied, "Not true."

"Really?"

A nod. "Honorable."

"But filled with rejects and outcasts." Omrak pounced on the unspoken confirmation.

Asin could only shrug at that.

"They never asked," Daniel said. "I don't think they're interested in me. Us."

"Interested." Asin pointed a finger at herself. "Asked."

"You didn't tell me?"

Asin shrugged. "Telling now."

Daniel sighed but let it go. They were certainly an option, as one of the larger guilds. A tier-two guild if you would, not the biggest but in some ways, with just as much political power. In other ways, much less since there was no such thing as a Beastkin noble. But in terms of sheer volume of members, they certainly were larger than even the Burning Fields.

"Fine. So that's six then." Daniel paused, doing the count again in his head. "Any idea how we'd choose?"

"Ask."

Omrak nodded in agreement to Asin's short answer. At their suggestion, Daniel made a face at being forced to talk to the guilds again but eventually nodded. "Fine. I'll see if we can set up appointments after our delve tomorrow.

"Now. About tomorrow's delve . . ."

***

Early the next morning, the group stood before the glowing doorway that led to the entrance of the Aramis Dungeon. Unlike Porthos, with its moving walkways, Aramis was a more difficult Dungeon in theory for Adventurers. At the Yellow-level, they were barely allowed into the first section of the Dungeon.

"Ready?" Daniel asked his friends. Like himself, the group were fully equipped. In his case, that meant a breastplate with pauldrons and bracers and a banded metal skirt along with his round shield, enchanted hammer, and loaded crossbow. He, of course, had his pot-helm on, covering his head with a simple woolen cap within to reduce friction and increase padding.

"Always, Friend Daniel. To glory we go!" Omrak said, answering immediately. The Northerner wore a simple, open-faced helm as well over his—finally enchanted—hardened leather jerkin and plated bracers. The jerkin was so long that it swept past his hips and was belted tight over his body with a large—and also enchanted—leather belt with loops for his throwing hatchets. Over his back, Omrak had fastened the scabbard for his greatsword, though he held the five-foot implement easily in his hands.

Asin was the least armored of the group, eschewing a helmet for a small round cap that helped cover the back and top of her head but left her ears free, wearing a light leather jacket and her signature red cloak. Criss-crossing her chest were multiple throwing knives, with two longer daggers belted at her hips and enchanted lightning bracers on her arms. The only other equipment she wore was an enchanted necklace of protection which she had upgraded recently to provide her even more security. It was a subtle spell, allowing shots to slide off her body rather than a hard defense like Daniel's shield.

All in all, the team had improved their overall equipment by dribs and drabs. Daniel had opted for simple, non-enchanted improvements for now, while Asin had gone the opposite direction and, rather than adding to her equipment, had instead focused on improving individual pieces. Still, Daniel could not help but reflect that compared to a couple of years ago, there was certainly a stark contrast.

In answer to Daniel's question, Asin offered the Adventurer a brief nod and together the group strode in, moments before the guard who had been waiting for them barked at them to get moving. Daniel had to admit, he understood the guard's impatience. Even if Aramis had multiple entrances, unlike most Dungeons, there was still a steady stream of Adventurers entering at this time of day.

Early morning sunlight gave way to the dim-blue lighting of Dungeon-illuminated walls. Carved walls and clean stone passages led off from the starting point which the team quickly vacated, moving confidently down one of the three hallways and clearing the way for other teams. Asin led the way, her head cocked to the side as she skipped past the marked traps that earlier teams had left behind, her nose twitching as she spotted the splash of blood where an unfortunate Adventurer missed a trap. However, the trap itself was gone, absorbed by the Dungeon for re-use somewhere deeper.

In short order, the team pulled away from the other teams and started slowing down, Asin leading the team unerringly away. In unexplored passages, she checked for traps, tossing the occasional weighted rock or rolling a sphere down the corridor in verification before moving forward.

Not long after they left the noise of traversed passages did they encounter their first monster.

The creature that trundled forwards was big, though not gigantic. Seven feet tall, its limbs were covered with fur, a stark contrast to its bare, scaled chest and beaked, front-facing and predatory eyes. The Adventurers Guild had named the creatures, uninspiringly, Swift Apes.

Suiting its actions to its name, the moment the Ape spotted the trio it bounded forward. Eschewing the use of a weapon, the Ape instead swung its arm down at the leading Beastkin. Asin snarled, throwing herself into a backflip, bouncing away even as Daniel angled his body to the side to fire his crossbow.

Just as the healer was pulling the trigger, a flare of magic rose up around them as the Swift Ape triggered its own elemental ability. Earth exploded from the ground, showering the dodging Catkin with dirt and making Daniel flinch a little. Pulled off its mark, the bolt flew through the air and tore a chunk of meat off the Ape's shoulder muscle, cauterizing the wound at the same time as Daniel's **Lesser Ring of Flame** imbued his attack with fiery damage.

"Earth-bound! I hate Earth-bound Apes," Omrak snarled as he rushed past Asin to meet the Ape. He swung his greatsword in a low, sweeping attack that the Ape blocked with its now earth-encrusted arms.

"You hate all elemental-bound apes," Daniel snarked, even as he worked to pull the crossbow string back. He grunted, his arm muscles straining as he nocked the string and then seated a crossbow bolt. In the corner of his eyes, he noted how Asin had thrown a couple of her knives, one of which now lodged in the Ape's thigh.

"That's. Because. They. Are. Annoying!" Each word was punctuated by a blow, blocked or thrown by the big Northerner. Yet, Omrak stayed light on his feet, quick to dodge aside when the Ape attempted another **Earth Eruption** attack.

As it reeled back, recovering from the expenditure of Mana and Stamina, Asin threw a knife, using **Fan of Knives** to split the attack. The multiplied knives dug into the creature, bolts of lightning racing across the monster's body as her enchanted lightning bracers carried their damage over. A moment later, Daniel's crossbow bolt impacted on the opposite shoulder, spinning the Ape around. The loud hiss of seared flesh and the screech of the monster told of the continued damage their enchantments lay upon it.

Injured, its body riddled with enchanted attacks, the Earth Swift Ape's end was guaranteed. Omrak quickly made work of the injured creature, while Daniel renocked his crossbow and watched for additional danger and Asin snuck around to threaten its flank. Not that Omrak needed the help, but the added distraction made the fight even simpler.

"Good stone," Omrak said, picking up the Mana stone that the disappearing body of the

Swift Ape deposited. Without comment, he tossed the stone over to Asin who caught and stored the stone for the team. "Are they becoming simpler, or is it just me?"

"We're learning," Daniel said. "Also, the enchantments make a big difference."

"True. I much prefer single or double opponents to the Imps," Omrak said.

"Easier Daniel hit," Asin said, grinning as she picked up and sheathed her knives.

"I'm getting better!" Daniel said. He didn't bother looking for his bolts. The negative of the **Lesser Flame** enchantment was that it damaged his bolts, making them unable to be reused. As for the metal within them, it was not worth the cost and time to search for the bolts. Better to leave it to the scavengers or the Dungeon. "Come on. I'd like to get to the fifth floor this time."

"The last time was not my fault!" Omrak said, though he followed after Asin once she returned to the front and scouted ahead. "Zarits swore that there was a hidden section on the third floor."

"That neither the Guild nor the maps have ever indicated," Daniel said. Not that he intended to rib the Northerner too much. After all, they had all agreed to go looking.

"Shhh!" Asin hissed at them as she bent over an unmarked trap, marking its location for others.

Grinning, the pair fell silent and focused. The first floor might not be much challenge, but it was better to be safe.

Chapter 4

"Twenty-four gold, eleven silver," Omrak read out proudly after being passed the tally note from Asin. For a single day's run, it was a good return, though they would have to spend some of it on consumables and fixing their equipment.

Asin nodded, pushing the pile of coins to each of the other two. She had no true fear about showing the coins here, in the Adventurers Guild's inn. The amount they were handling was a decent haul, but nothing spectacular and certainly nothing that another Adventurer would chance being thrown out for. As for Pickpockets and common Thieves, the Adventurers Guild's attendants were all on the lookout for them, leaving only the truly foolhardy to try their hand at stealing from Adventurers within the Guild itself.

Even so, her friends quickly picked up and stored the coins in their inventory, putting them away before anyone had a good chance to look them over. Asin nodded, grateful that they had the sense to do that. No need to tempt others more than necessary.

"Note." Asin next handed Daniel a rolled-up slip of paper. When he unrolled it, she curiously peered over, only to see a list of names and times. She absently nodded to herself, having guessed that it would be replies to his earlier queries.

A familiar set of approaching footsteps made the Catkin turn her head, peering curiously as the Guildmistress of the Bent Nail trooped over, flanked by a pair of her teammates. Unlike her provocative evening clothing, Nicole was clad in full plate armor and bearing her weapons. Even from a few feet away, Asin could smell the lingering traces of blood and stink of fear and adrenaline on the party's skin.

"Daniel, Asin, Omrak." She greeted the trio by name, a smile splitting her face.

"Guildmistress Novak," Omrak replied, turning slightly to smile at the young ladies. One sniffed, turning away from the Northerner whose smile slipped for a fraction of a second before returning. "Brandi. Adelle. A pleasure to see you this evening, as always."

And evening it was, with the noise of returning workmen and Adventurers and the aroma of roasting meat for supper filtering in from the streets outside. Being late winter, even as far south as they were in Brad, the light had begun to dim as the sun set. Within though, Mana lamps kept the Adventurers Guild brightly lit. An easy cost to bear, when the Guild was the only official way to sell Mana stones.

The thought had Asin flicking open her inventory briefly peering at the few stones she'd kept to sell to her contacts. Of course, she would make sure the team received their share later, but cutting out the middleman increased their take by twenty to thirty percent. A good trade, if dangerous, since doing so was a fineable offence.

"—finally got our potions, so we'll be delving deep tomorrow," Nicole was saying, answering Daniel's question. She took a seat beside him, sitting with a slight hitch in her movements as she finished lowering herself the last few inches.

"Problem?" Daniel said, frowning.

Asin let out a little chuff of amusement, her tail lashing behind her. Did he still not notice how some of these "friends" only showed up to speak with them when they were hurt? Nothing serious, of course, but just enough that a quick **Healer's Mark** spell would fix it.

"I'm fine. Just a small pull," Nicole said, waving her hand away. "I actually wanted to speak with you about something else."

"Oh?" Daniel's eye still lingered on her body before he wrenched it up, even as the rest of the table fell silent.

"I heard a rumor you were asking to meet with some guilds."

"That's right," Daniel said, warily.

Asin picked up her cup, sipping at the mulled wine within. She preferred chabu, but they did not serve it here. Or when they did bring in a barrel, charged twice the going rate. Using the edge of the cup to hide her face, Asin cast her gaze around, spotting how a few nearby tables were now paying attention. She even saw a Goatkin the table over leering at them, its ears cocked in their direction.

Daniel always missed these things, more focused on what was in front of him than potential threats behind. He was too straightforward, too good. But he was a healer, and his Gift left him vulnerable. It was her job to keep him safe out here, just like it was his in the Dungeon.

"I'm a little hurt you didn't invite us," Nicole said, fluttering her eyes a little.

"Well, that, uhhh . . ." Daniel paused.

Before he could make an offer or suggest that he forgot or squirreled out of it, Asin spoke up. "Small."

"Pardon?" Nicole said, frowning a little.

"Guild small," Asin repeated, offering a slight tilt of her head downwards and lowering her ears to show it was not personal. Of course, she wasn't certain Nicole would understand the body language, but it was worth the shot. They did have a trio of Beastkin in their group, even if one was a Dogkin.

"Well, we're not that small . . ." Nicole said.

Daniel shot a glance at Asin, one mixed between relief and disapproval at her being so blunt. But, his hand forced, he backed her up like he always did. "No, you're not. But you're not really a regional guild. Or national. And that's what we need."

"Oh." Nicole paused, her gaze sweeping over Daniel as she considered her next words. Eventually, she smiled. "Well, I hope we can still rely on you for the occasional consultation?"

"Uhhh, I guess?" Daniel shrugged. "I think it'd depend on the guild."

"Of course, of course," Nicole replied immediately. She shifted slightly, wincing again. Daniel's eyes drifted over, and Asin could not help but roll her eyes. Especially when he made the low-voiced offer and Nicole gladly accepted.

Not that Asin had much to object to, other than his good nature being taken advantage of. It was not as if Nicole did not return the favor at times, between hints and recommendations for the levels they went to as well as merchant and trader recs. Since both she and Omrak had already been healed and they would be calling it a night, Daniel's Mana would regenerate by the time they entered the Dungeon the next day. If he didn't heal her, he'd probably just go to the hospice and do some healing there before the night was over.

Still, Asin kept an ear out, watched as he cast the spell, watched how they talked to him. And eventually, listened as they got around to giving advice.

"Make sure to go down with them. You'll want to see in-person how they train their teams, how they teach and deploy their people," Nicole was saying. "It's not enough to just, you know, be told what they do. You need to see it."

"So, down into the Dungeons with them?" Daniel said.

Asin found herself nodding to their words, grateful for Nicole's recommendations. She continued to list and point out things the party needed to know, questions to ask, playing advisor to the newbies now that they were certain that they weren't going to pick their guild.

Sometimes, Asin had to admit, Daniel's tendency to heal first and talk later worked out well.

***

The first to meet with them was Gadi, the vice-guildmaster of the Seven Stones. Unlike many others, Gadi himself rarely entered the Dungeon these days, being semi-retired. He had been what was termed a Sword-Mage, a multi-Class Adventurer who had attempted to specialize in both magic and his weapon.

Of course, because of the slow regeneration of Mana, every mage learned a few melee or ranged skills. But most did so only to protect themselves, and to offer some small level of support to their team. Ranged weaponry were the most common choices since it allowed the mage to stay safely back while adding another ranged attacker to the team's arsenal.

Even so, ranged weaponry was less effective in many Dungeons. Cramped passages, tight corners, and shortened sightlines meant that ranged attacks were less useful in many levels. But not all. And realistically, most parties were happy to get any mage on their team, since their versatility and added magical damage could make the difference in clearing certain levels or failure.

Even so, few mages took it to the same extent as Gadi where they devoted significant portions of their time learning a melee weapon and added themselves to the frontline. Most mages were too studious; the rigors of magical enchantment and casting requiring long hours of book study and practice. Splitting time off to study weaponry as well resulted in the same problem that both Daniel and Gadi faced. Barring being a prodigy in both areas, at some point, one's skill in one area of your study would lag. For Daniel, his melee combat skills lagged far behind his healing ability. For Gadi, his magic skills had fallen by the wayside as he studied the sword.

But at the higher-leveled Dungeons, those ranked Expert and above, specialists were of greater use. A single, powerful Mage could end a Boss fight before it began in earnest, saving lives. A strong expert swordsman could deal damage and cripple multiple monsters in a fight, dealing damage or holding their attention. Unfortunately, Sword-Mages could do a little of both, but neither well. And it was because of this that it was rumored that Gadi had failed, eventually being sidelined and forced to take an administrative post.

All this, Omrak related to Daniel as they walked over to the Seven Stones guildhall, waving his hands around in an expansive manner to punctuate his comments. "—and that's why I think you should be careful yourself, Friend Daniel. For you are not spending time bettering your weapon skills. You lack even a powerful melee skill."

"I have **Perin's Blow**," Daniel said. He hopped over a splotch of manure and landed on the rough-fitted cobblestone street, barely even noticing the waste. It would be picked up soon enough by the collectors or the street children, all intent on making a copper from the valuable fertilizer.

"Yes. And combined with your **Find Weakness** Skill, it can injure or end an already injured opponent. But compare that to **Thundering Strike**," Omrak said.

Daniel grunted. "That's a bit of a cheating skill though . . ."

"Nothing cheating about it," Omrak said. "It is a powerful skill because I have gained much experience. It focuses my attack on a single point and adds the strength of the sky to it."

"I did wonder why it's not called **Lightning Strike**," Daniel said.

"Another skill," Asin piped up. "Fast." She jabbed her hand out, miming the skill activation.

"Like **Snake Strike**?" Daniel said.

"Faster."

"Huh." Daniel shook his head. Sometimes, it seemed that Eris had gone for the simplistic in the naming of skills. But perhaps that was for the best. Too many Adventurers spent more time at the training pells than studying books. "But Asin is missing a sure-kill skill."

In reply, Asin grinned at Daniel.

"Wait, you have one?"

A nod. Asin dodged sideways, getting out of the way of an older laundrywoman and her large bag that she was hauling to the river. That put her up against the whitewashed walls of the shop, getting an irate rebuke from the shopkeeper as he spotted the Beastkin. With practiced ease, the group ignored him as they kept walking.

"What?"

"I am curious too, Friend Asin."

"**Penetrator**."

"Huh?"

"Ah, a good passive skill. Not the same, but at higher levels." Omrak paused, raised an eyebrow, and got a nod from Asin. "It begins to show its value. Especially if you combine that with your other skills like **Bone Breaker**. An interesting combination."

"I don't get it," Daniel said, turning his head between the pair of melee fighters.

"**Penetrator**—or **Penetration**—is a skill that comes from the combination of perception, monster biology and weapon skills. Once you achieve sufficient levels, it is available for purchase," Omrak said. "As a combined skill, it is hard to level, but it has the benefit of also being an on-going passive. All of Friend Asin's attacks will dig deeper, do more damage. And at higher levels, it should penetrate deep within.

"It is a skill for precision fighters."

Before Daniel could inquire further—especially on the part about monster biology—the trio arrived before the door to the Seven Stones Guild. The healer looked up, taking in the squat, two-story whitewashed building and could not help but compare it to the others beside it. They were in the richer part of town—thus the paved stones and recently whitewashed walls—and thus everything from the trim to the clay-fired tiling on the roof itself was well kept. Yet there were little signs of disrepair to Daniel's eyes, little indications that while organisation might be rich—comparatively—they were not affluent.

"Well, are we to enter?" Omrak said, suddenly looking nervous. He tugged on his tunic, his best set of three and the one he wore most often when he went out on dates. It was a little thinner, a little tighter woven than his other rougher, much-patched wear he wore into the Dungeon.

Not that Daniel had anything to comment on Omrak's clothing choices. He too wore his best outfit, but unlike Omrak, he had a wider range of clothing options to choose from. One of the advantages of being a healer in the hospice was that he often received small gifts. In this case, the shirt he wore was a hand-me-down from a grateful patient. It was much finer quality than Omrak's own tunic, but his was about twenty years out of style.

"Yes," Daniel said.

Of course, rather than barging in, he knocked on the door before shifting on his feet, taking a few seconds to clean his boots on the edge of the upraised lip of the door. Like most of the other buildings on the street, to get to the door, you had to ascend a few steps to reach it, offering the inside of the house a little protection from the constant rains and mud.

Asin, beside him, was already cleaning her own sandals. While she preferred walking barefoot whenever possible, the city streets were not on that list. If nothing else, the constant rumbling carts and deposits and the need to keep her feet clean on entering a residence meant footwear was a necessity.

As he was watching the Catkin, Daniel noticed the way her head tilted; her ears swiveled moments before he too heard the footsteps from within the guild hall. A moment later, the door creaked open to reveal Gadi himself, the short, five-foot human glaring up at the group.

"So, you finally chose to speak with me, did you? What happened? The Burning Fields turn you down?" he said, crossing his arms before himself. Dark blonde hair, nearly brown in the dim lighting shone, though from their angle, Daniel spotted the thinning center line.

"We have chosen to explore other options first," Daniel said. "As you said, they're a little large. And might not offer what we want."

Gadi's eyes narrowed for a second before he nodded, waving the group through the door. Once they were in and the door closed, Gadi led them to the sitting room on the door's left. As they walked forward, Daniel could not help but notice the doors at the end of the hallway that led out to the training grounds.

The sitting room itself contained simple carpets and wall hangings, a cabinet filled with glassware and drinks, and a series of wooden lounging chairs. Gadi took the single seat, plopping himself down with force before he faced the group.

"So, you recall my offer, yes?" he declared beforehand, before continuing. "What else do you want?"

"Remind me," Omrak called out. "I have forgotten what it was you offered us."

"I offered the *healer* a salary, a silver for his healing services and double shares on any delve. As well as the usual benefits of being part of our guild—access to our merchant and alchemical resources and the guild library."

"And us?" Asin asked, perched as she was on a chair.

Gadi glanced at the Beastkin before he turned away with a dismissive sneer and faced Daniel again. "I can take in your friends. They are unremarkable, but not useless. But we'll want to add to your party. It is significantly under-strength."

"I'd like to choose my members," Daniel said.

"We'll send who we have, but you have to take at least five down with you," Gadi said. "We won't let our investment die just because he didn't take enough precautions."

"That's fine. But I won't work with people who I don't trust," Daniel said.

"Of course," Gadi said. "And as I said, your friends are adequate. Would you like to see your potential teammates now?"

"They're here?" Daniel said, surprised.

"Mmm . . . we have some. The ones missing a team," Gadi said. "And one other Advanced team, who are spending the day training. We institute a five-two regime."

"Five-two?" Omrak said, frowning. The big Northerner was lounging in the room, having made the couch he had taken his own. The ostentatious display seemed to not make him unconscious at all, unlike Asin.

"Five days training, two days delving," Gadi replied.

"Not the other way around?" Daniel said.

Daniel's reply had Gadi bark a laugh, one that was closer to the bray of a mule than a human chuckle. Catching himself, he stared at Daniel before he snorted. "Who goes delving five days in a row?"

Asin let out a chuff of laughter, while Omrak frowned. When Gadi looked at the group, frowning, Daniel explained. "We do."

"What? Why? How do you . . ." Gadi paused, then shook his head. "Of course. Healer. You overuse your skill on them, don't you?"

"I keep the team well healed."

"And subject their body to repeated healings," Gadi said, shaking his head. "You should not."

"Why?"

"Repeated magical healing can cause issues in the long-term. It's a known issue with older Adventurers. Certain kinds of diseases that erupt, causing tumors and other issues," Gadi said.

"Oh, that!" Daniel nodded. He knew about those issues. In fact, they treated cases like that in the hospice relatively regularly. Of course, Gadi was not correct in calling it a disease since it was not an external effect on the body but a problem within the body itself. Daniel could— and did—scan his friends and himself for the issue. It was a weird problem, one that could easily be fixed by his Gift for minimal cost when it first started showing up but was extremely expensive later on. It was one of the few things he refused to fix when presented to him, instead reverting to alchemical concoctions. Sometimes, those even worked.

"That." Gadi's eyes narrowed, and Daniel smiled brightly in turn. Soon enough, he'd learn the truth if he hadn't already, but it was better to not speak of it just yet. "Well, so long as your friends and teammates understand the dangers."

"I don't heal everything," Daniel said, nodding. "It's good for the body to heal by itself at times. Magical healing just resets the body, instead of letting it grow."

At least most kinds.

Healer's Mark was more a regeneration spell, which just sped up the body's own natural healing properties. It actually had less chance of causing issues, though for some reason, some individuals were more prone to damage than others. Interestingly, it had nothing to do with Constitution itself. Of course, there were true

Healers who spent their time researching the why, but much of it was still speculative. Common theories ranged from Erlis's will, to unseen diseases, to intrinsic issues within an individual's body. That such problems were more common among inbred creatures led credence to the first and last theories.

And outside of the low-level spells like **Healer's Mark**, there were more powerful healing spells like **the Body's Return** and **Regeneration** as well as the priest's blessings like **Erlis's Forgiveness** that sidestepped issues like that entirely. Either by forcing the body to regenerate or that flooded the body with a purer form of Mana—or perhaps, a better controlled use of Mana; the priests were rather ambiguous about that point—that not only healed and regenerated but cleared the body of other issues.

"Good. It's still dangerous to push like that," Gadi said.

"People," Asin said, butting in and tapping the table with a clawed finger.

Gadi frowned, eyeing the spot where Asin had tapped as if he was distrustful that she might have damaged it, before sighing. "Yes, yes. I'll get them." He paused. "Or we could join them."

"Join?" Asin cocked her head to the side.

"On the training grounds."

The enthusiastic nods from the group had Gadi smiling as he stood up and waved them to follow him. Daniel could not help but grin a little, anticipation rising. There was definitely something to be said about watching his potential allies at work.

And really, Omrak was not wrong. He did need to work on his skills.

Chapter 5

The training yard that Daniel had spotted at the back of the building was larger than he had expected. Contrary to his expectations, it actually took up the entirety of the neighbors' yards too, making the entire thing at least two hundred feet wide and another sixty feet long. The Seven Stones had made good use of the additional space, splitting the area into a couple of fighting rings, a physical exercise section, a walled-off portion where a pair of Adventurers practiced their archery, and the largest area—a magical arena.

Large as the training yard was, it was crowded too with multiple members of the Seven Stones Guild working. The dueling rings were in use, with a small crowd of watchers armored up observing the combat. An older Adventurer limped between the two rings, calling out commentary as she moved. Even from here, Daniel could feel the subtle tug of her skill, as her **Trainer's Voice** sped up skill improvement.

In the main arena, a team moved through the rocky terrain, climbing up the boulders and edging along the pathways that had been created as they warily searched for their targets.

It was Asin, from the team's vantage point, that spotted their opponents first. She pointed them out while speaking. "Kobolds."

Daniel frowned as he stared at the group of long-limbed, thin creatures that were flooding out of a small opening in the ground. They hissed a little at the bright lights but jabbered to one another as they spread out from the entrance. Unlike the monsters they had fought, these Kobolds carried real weapons—short, bronze daggers—and wore stitched together hide.

"What . . . ?"

"We find it's better for our trainees to fight real monsters once in a while," Gadi said. "We purchase captured monsters and have them brought over."

"Kobolds are real?" Daniel said.

"Native to Khash," Gadi said.

Daniel frowned, staring as the group of Kobolds began sending out scouting parties. They communicated more than they had in the Dungeon, calling out to one another as they travelled forth. Since the arena itself was not too large, the adventuring team and the first of the scouting parties found each other soon enough.

"Are they . . . sapient?" Daniel said, hesitantly.

"As much as goblins are," Gadi replied. "In fact, they are, in many ways, the Khash equivalent of our Goblins. Monstrous, constantly breeding and eating. Irrationally aggressive." As he finished speaking, the Kobolds launched themselves at the better armed Adventurers with a screech, wielding their weapons with vigor if not much skill. "Utterly impossible to work with."

"Still . . . to capture them . . ." Daniel frowned. It twigged at his conscience a little. Killing them was messy—especially these non-

Dungeon versions, where their bodies lay on the ground rather than dispersing in motes of Mana—but understandable. Monsters were monsters. But trapping them for this . . .

"It's good training." Gadi eyed Daniel, the short vice-guildmaster's lip thinning in consideration. "We don't stint on our training budget."

"I guess." Daniel fell silent, watching as the adventuring team finished killing off the scout team and followed the tracks back to the main group. There, the Kobolds had regrouped into a large mass, waiting just outside of where the rocks converged with the goal of luring out the team and using their greater numbers. Unfortunately, their hesitation worked to their detriment as a young girl stepped out from behind the team, raising her hand and chanting a series of words before she released a swirling mass of air.

The spell struck the center of the Kobold group, just above the short creatures' heads and exploded with a terrifying, ear-aching shriek. The Kobolds, with their larger ears and at the epicenter of the blast were lashed by the exploding wind and tossed aside by the exploding wall of sound.

"**Sonic Ball**," Gadi said, rubbing at his ears. "Lady Nyssa is one of those we would have you meet. She is a powerful Mage but thus far has yet to click with any team."

Into that disorganized mob, the rest of the team rushed in, even as the archer at the top of the rock outcropping loosed his arrows to target any Kobold still standing and attempting to organize their friends. The remainder of the battle was soon over, only for the team to turn around and shout at the Mage, hands waving and gesturing, though only muted words reached the group.

"**Sound Barrier**," Gadi explained when Omrak asked. "We keep one active over the arena whenever Lady Nyssa is training."

"They look unhappy with her," Daniel said.

"Powerful. More powerful," Asin said, then mimed the explosion with her hands. "Hurt ears."

"Yes. It seems she leveled her spell again and did not inform her team," Gadi said with a sigh. The only one, Daniel noted, who was not shouting at her but was watching the team below with an arrow nocked to his bow. "The archer of that group," Gadi continued, "is part of the Lady's group and her Loyal Bodyguard. He is also deaf."

Daniel blinked, but nodded. That would explain why he seemed to be unaffected by the attack and was watching the entire thing as though he was ready to defend his "lady."

"Well, we shall let them settle matters first," Gadi said, smiling at the group. "There are a few others to introduce you to. Now, in the dueling rings, we have . . ."

Gesturing the team over, Gadi brought the group over. Bemused, Daniel followed along.

***

"Zef." The scaled drake offered his hand to Daniel to shake. Wielding a long spear, the drake was only one of three Beastkin in the Seven Stones Guild that Daniel could spot. "Spear-wielder. Front-line fighter. I specialize in high damage elemental attacks."

After letting go of Daniel's hand, he grabbed his spear from his other hand, spun, and threw it. The spear arced through the air, burst into light, and pierced one of the target pells on the other side of the training ground. It lodged halfway through the pell and burst out the back at the "Return" command Zef hissed.

Catching the weapon with one hand, he continued. "I have some ranged expertise as well."

"I see . . ." Daniel said, eyeing the shattered pell and gulping a little. That was incredibly high damage for a single attack.

Omrak, beside Daniel, nodded approvingly.

<hr>

***

"You're a healer? Do you know, I've had this pain in the back of my knee for weeks now," the shifty-eyed, spiky-haired, and pale-faced speaker blathered on. "Do you think you could . . ."

"If Adventurer Chai decides to join us, his services will be available to all Guild members," Gadi said. "As is Priest Yorrick's right now as you know, Harlow."

"Yeah, but that Priest stares at me and lectures me all the time." Harlow shifted slightly. "And Daniel is right here. . . . He's not using that Mana of his right now, right? So it'd be a small thing . . ."

"If you stopped stealing and repented, perhaps Priest Yorrick . . ."

"Lies! I've stolen nothing," Harlow protested.

"And Merchant Sherz's recent visit?" Gadi glared.

"Well, okay. I might have taken an apple . . ." At Gadi's gaze, Harlow muttered, "And a coin or two . . . but a man's got to keep his hand in!"

Asin beside the group just shook her head. Gadi, spotting Asin's reaction, dismissed Harlow before he continued. "Harlow is one of our most talented rogues—a former thief, burglar, and cutpurse, he has a second sense for traps and danger. He also has the **Blueprint Skill**, which is similar to the **Mapmaking Skill**, but more specialized for internal locations. Including Dungeons."

"He's also a thief," Daniel said.

"He doesn't steal from the Guild," Gadi said, even though his smile was a little strained. "He's also found at least four secret rooms and locations in eleven delves."

Asin's ears swiveled forward in interest while Omrak frowned. Daniel just rolled his eyes as Gadi led them over to their next target.

***

The flame-haired teenager let out a breath then released the arrow, watching it strike the target. She grinned to herself, turning the curved bow she held in her hand sideways as she began nocking another arrow. Gadi cleared his throat another time, making her jump a little and flush. As she did so, the fine freckles on her pale skin stood out more.

"Vice-guildmaster! Sorry. Sorry. I didn't see you there," she cried out, almost dropping the arrow she held as she bowed and tried to put the arrow away at the same time. Eventually, she got things settled, staring at the rest of the group inquisitively.

"You must work on your battlefield awareness," Gadi said. "Put more points in **Perception** next time, Anne."

"Yes, sir!" Anne bobbed a nod again. "I . . . are these new recruits?"

Gadi turned, making quick introductions before he continued. "Daniel here is a talented healer. Anne is an Adventurer, with a minor non-Combat Class. She is young, having just graduated from our Beginner's training program but has indicated a desire to pursue healing as a secondary skill."

"Really?" Daniel said, eyeing the tight cluster of arrows around the bullseye of the target. "That's admirable. It's a lot of study."

"Yes, sir!"

Daniel frowned at being called a sir. He wasn't that much older than the teenager. Though . . . maybe he was? She was only sixteen or so.

"I've been reading a lot. About herbs. And common cures."

"Reading isn't enough," Daniel said with a frown. "Have you been practicing?"

"Only the basics of binding wounds and the like," Anne said. "The teams won't let me do much more. And Priest Yorrick deals with everything else, though he lets me watch." She perked up at the end.

Daniel shook his head. "You should work in the local hospices. We can always use another pair of hands, and you'll learn faster. There are Nurses who can provide you information too."

"I want to be a Healer, not a Nurse. And why do I need to know how to deal with toothaches and colds?" Anne said, crossing her arms. "I wish to be an Adventuring Healer, a Combat Medic!"

"Adventurer Anne!" Gadi snapped. The young Adventurer flushed, bowing low and muttering apologies. "Adventurer Chai is providing you his expertise. Thank him for that and then run a dozen laps in apology."

She flushed red but did as Gadi said even as Daniel continued to mutter about how it was unnecessary.

As she scrambled away, Gadi rolled his eyes. "Youngsters."

"Forsooth," Omrak said, nodding wisely.

Asin, behind, choked a little.

***

More Adventurers and adventuring teams. In the end, Daniel and team begged off, escaping the enthusiastic introductions and Gadi's explanation of the various features of the guild house and the benefits of joining the Seven Stones.

Outside the building, on the busy, paved streets, Daniel drew a deep breath and looked up. The afternoon sun had slipped past its zenith and was now hidden behind the buildings around them, leaving the streets themselves shadowed in the fading light. Already, lamplighters were bringing out the Mana-stone charged lanterns that decked the streets while crowds of servants hurried home after being released for the day. Only the richest houses would keep their servants working through the night, as few could work without sufficient light.

"What do you think?" Daniel said finally, as he dragged his team away.

"They are very enthusiastic," Omrak said, recalling the numerous individuals they'd spoken to. Many who'd offered to bring them with them.

"New," Asin said.

"But do you think it's worth joining?" Daniel could not help but ask.

"We'll see, in a few days, won't we?" Omrak said, grinning.

The last thing they'd done before leaving the guild house was to arrange to accompany the Seven Stones into Aramis in a few days. The new team—one made up of enthusiastic, potential members and a few more mature ones—would showcase the guild's training methods. Including their ability to quickly integrate disparate team members.

Or so Gadi had assured them.

"I guess we will," Daniel said.

He sighed, rubbing at his neck. They'd find out soon enough. Tomorrow, they'd enter the Dungeon again themselves, before swinging by the day after to visit another guild. Hopefully, meeting with each of the other guilds would not take a whole day.

Chapter 6

Daniel watched the three Swift Apes and the Swift Ape Boss in the distance the next day, his body lowered close to the ground while he clutched his crossbow. He could not help but reflect on how different these Dungeon-formed monsters were compared to the Kobolds he had seen the day before.

Unlike the Kobolds, these monsters rarely spoke. In fact, they rarely varied in their motion. The Swift Ape Boss sat silently, staring into space while the other monsters moved in predictable patterns around the cavern that housed them. While they attempted to mimic life, the Mana stones that powered them could only hold so much Mana, basically giving them only a certain amount of autonomy. Of course, Daniel knew that the lower one went, the more complicated and powerful were the Mana stones that generated these creatures, resulting in an increase in the creature's intelligence.

But these creatures? They were nothing more than automata—clockwork creatures. Simplistic monsters that reacted in well-known ways. They attacked, aggressively, because they were programmed to do so. Sometimes, they might even act like living creatures, but only at first glance.

"Can we do it?" Omrak asked, staring at the group. He was crouched over Daniel, supporting himself against the wall with one hand while the other clutched his greatsword.

"It's only four of them," Daniel said. "If we can lure them into the corridor, we should be fine." He looked up, staring at the ceiling and then pulled back as he turned to Asin. "Could you climb up?"

"Ceiling strike?" Asin said.

Daniel nodded. In a few short words, the plan was set. A few minutes later, with Asin and Omrak in position, Daniel slipped out to the corridor, dropping the trio of bolts he'd withdrawn from his quiver onto the ground and raising his weapon. For a precious few seconds, the creatures did not notice him. Seconds that Daniel used to line up his shot.

Finally, one of the Swift Apes spotted the Adventurer, letting out a howl that alerted the other guards. As one, the guards started charging over while the Boss slowly roused itself. Daniel ignored the commotion, making sure his shot was perfectly lined up before pulling the trigger gently.

The bolt launched itself from his crossbow with a twang, jerking him back a little as it released its spent energy. He immediately began hauling back on the string, barely paying attention to his attack. Thankfully, the corridor itself was straight and narrow, leaving Daniel only a little space to focus upon and miss. And this time, he didn't, the bolt sinking deep into the leading Swift Ape's torso.

Daniel kept firing, ignoring the thudding of his heart, the slight iron tang on the back of his tongue as his adrenaline spiked as the monsters charged. He focused, getting off two more shots before the monsters arrived and he was forced to store his crossbow bolt and raise his shield.

His efforts had borne bloody fruit though, leaving the first Swift Ape sprawled on the ground, twitching as its life blood flowed out of it. The second monster, leaping at Daniel, was met by a wide sweeping attack by Omrak that as much batted it away as it tore through its tough skin and fur. This gave Daniel sufficient time to arm himself, raising mace and shield to follow behind the already charging Omrak. Together, they engaged the third Swift Ape, while the fourth was dispatched by Asin, who'd dropped onto the rearguard with her daggers extended. She stabbed into its shoulders, riding the monster down and ending its life, her weapon seeking lungs and heart as she sprawled on top of it.

By the time Daniel and Omrak finished their pair of attackers, the Swift Ape Boss had charged down the corridor, engaging Asin. The fast-moving creature had forced the normally agile Catkin to fight in close combat where lightning from its attacks and hers mixed, sparking in the sky. Asin, not having the creature's natural resistance, was faring badly and receiving the worst of it, her fur standing on end, doubling the size of the slim Beastkin as she sought escape.

"*To me*!" Omrak shouted, his voice echoing down the hallway, supported by his skill **Challenge of the North**. Forced by the magic of the skill, the Swift Ape Boss turned away from the slumping Catkin to charge Omrak.

Behind Omrak and to his off-hand's side, Daniel stared at the monster, his eyes narrowing. He searched for weaknesses, that innate understanding of locations to attack. His instincts, guided by the skill, offered little new information, however, nothing that multiple expeditions had not already gleaned. Lower right torso—liver. Side of the knees—to cripple. And a location just below the jaw hinge where a cluster of nerves lived.

As it bounded closer, the Swift Ape Boss drew its hand back and threw it forward. A burst of lightning arced forward, striking Omrak's raised greatsword and then the Northerner.

"Aaargh!" Omrak screamed, his body smoking red and grey. The damage from the attacks triggered his skill, the **Rage of the North**, giving him strength and allowing him to ignore the stunning effect of the attack, letting him skewer the monster's swinging other hand.

A twist of his torso, a ripping motion tore his sword free, half-severing the attacking arm. A pair of throwing knives bloomed in the back of the Swift Ape Boss, while Daniel stepped forward and low, triggering **Double Strike** to layer multiple attacks on the monster's moving feet. The first glanced off the knee, the second hammering into the thigh, slowing the monster down.

But for all their successful attacks, this was an Advanced Class Dungeon Boss. It would not fall so easily. Blocking an attack with his shield,

Daniel snarled and kept his head down, searching for an opening even as Omrak continued his attacks.

They would win. That, Daniel was certain of. It would just cost them in blood and pain.

***

Hours later, the team ascended from the Dungeon's portal, moving quickly under the eyes of the City Guards. Omrak grinned, stretching a little even as he felt the soreness of the day's activities. As he walked out of the passageway that housed the exit portal, he tilted his head around to take in the defensive walls that had been built around the Dungeon to spot the edges of the colorful setting sun.

"We did well today, honored friends!" Omrak rumbled.

He was not even exaggerating, for they had made it down to the fifth floor, an increase of a single level but one that brought them to a new biome. More than that, Omrak marveled at the increase in his Level and the new feeling of strength that permeated his body. As always, he'd dedicated his points immediately into his three physical attributes, with the focus upon **Constitution** and **Strength**.

As for his Skill Point, he would take a little longer to look it over. Probably tonight. While his initial plan was to increase his **Thunderous Strike** ability, increasing the amount of damage he could deal against a single opponent, it would be worthwhile to look at both his **Lightning's Call** ability and any new Skill Proficiency option. He had continued to improve his skill with the greatsword and dodge, as well as his proficiency in medium armors.

Not that he expected much addition, but Omrak was cognizant of his role as the main threat. Being able to deal with multiple enemies was just as important as killing a single, powerful attacker. And part of doing so was the ability to survive. So any additional skill that could help with that had to be considered greatly.

"Yes, we did," Daniel said, clapping Omrak on the shoulder.

Omrak grinned, then limped forward, joining the flow of Adventurers out of the gate. There were no major injuries today, and so he had refused the use of Daniel's spell. Better to ache a little now than to waste Daniel's Mana. It was not as if the pain was unusual, and it actually helped Omrak improve his **Pain Resistance** skill. More importantly, the Mana that Daniel saved could be used for others more in need later that night.

"Friend Asin," Omrak said, once they were out on the streets and away from the main flow of traffic. He tilted his head to the side, while continuing to speak. "Will you pass me the funds tomorrow? I have another matter to tend to."

"Oh? Hot date?" Daniel said, giving Omrak a big grin.

Sometimes, Omrak wondered about Daniel. While Omrak did indulge more than the healer—who, considering the sheer volume of offers he received and he accepted, could be considered almost prudish—it was as though he was entirely focused on those matters, unlike some other Adventurers.

"No, Friend Daniel. There is a small personal matter to attend to," Omrak said.

He waved goodbye to the pair, not wishing to explain further and headed away, leaving them to deal with the administrative matters. Once he reached the nearest cross-street, the big Northerner sped up, widening his stride and passing others by. He had multiple errands to run, including sending off further funds to be saved by his family. They, in turn, bought land and reared his sheep for him—for a price—and helped guarantee his eventual triumphant return.

But that was just a small matter for today. His bigger concern was making sure he made it out of the city and on time. It was good that they had managed to make it out early this time, or he would have had to hire a courier or even a horse to arrive on time.

After leaving his funds and receiving the simple runic script that marked the receipt by the House of Jarl—the largest merchant house in the north—Omrak strode out of the eastern gates of Silverstone. He kept to the far left of the path, hurrying in ground-eating strides as day slowly died. Even as the sun faded, the moons were already high in the sky, offering ample radiance. As for bandits, this close to the city, it was unlikely. Nor were they likely to bother one carrying a weapon like his so obviously.

In the meantime, Omrak pulled up the options for his new skill proficiencies. Like he had expected, he had a few new ones to consider.

Medium Armor – Subtle Movements

Shift your body subtly when receiving attacks, allowing dead-on strikes to glance aside and glancing strikes to slide away.

Skill: Passive

Cost: N/A

Effect: Reduces damage received by 3–7%. Amount reduced varies depending on number of attackers and attack.

It was not a dodge skill, but a damage mitigation skill. The advantage of the skill was that it was a passive skill, requiring none of Omrak's precious Stamina. But the amount reduced was minimal—at least on first purchase. Omrak understood that such a skill, with repeated purchases, could make him significantly sturdier. Even so, a better skill would be a **Damage Reflection** skill. Nicole had mentioned it to him previously, and it was one that she herself used. Coupled with expensive— and sturdy—enchanted armor, one could take attacks head on with minimal pain and reflect such attacks back to their opponent. This skill would make such a strategy less effective.

Moving on, Omrak looked at his next new Skill Proficiency.

Rage to Blood

A Northerner's famed rage and their immense survivability come from many areas including significant obstinance and this skill blessing.

Skill: Active

Cost: 30 Rage

Effect: Heal self for 10 Health over 3 seconds.

This was a bloodline blessing, one that came from his mixed, specialized Class—Northern Adventurer—rather than the pure Adventurer Class people like Daniel carried. It was only available to those who had Lund's Blessing, and as such, was a restricted Class. In the Beastkin states, other Beastkin adventuring bloodlines were available, though he knew that Asin herself had no opportunity to gain it.

It was a mixed matter, having a bloodline ability. It offered certain skills that were not available to normal Adventurers but also restricted other skills. Still, it was what Omrak had, and he would not bemoan his fate.

Even if Omrak had to admit to himself, he'd begun to question the sanity of taking on injuries just to use a Skill to regain health later. It was a powerful skill, and it would have been one he would have taken undoubtedly if he did not have the support of Daniel. The healer's ability was significantly more powerful than this skill.

"How far to the city, friend?" a voice called out, breaking Omrak from his musings.

He blinked, a hand creeping to his hatchets before the teenager relaxed, smiling at the family, the father carrying his child on his shoulders.

"Just another half-hour," Omrak called.

"Are there inns beside the gate? Or will we have to camp out?" the father asked, his gaze flicking over to a nearby stand of trees not far from the road.

"No need to camp. The gates of Silverstone stand open through the night," Omrak replied, smiling. "You'll find it safer within." Glancing up at the frowning little girl, Omrak continued. "Though the countryside around Silverstone is quite safe."

"Ah . . ." The mother looked relieved, shifting the pack on her shoulders. "Thank you, good sir."

Waving goodbye to the family, Omrak continued to hurry on. As much as he wanted to speak, he still had to finish his selection and reach the site of the ceremony. It would be an insult to Lund to arrive late.

Omrak quickly considered the rest of his options. **Thundering Strike II** and the **Lightning's Call II** were upgrades that were straightforward additional damage. It was not particularly innovative, but both skills had great use to him. Which was why they were in contention, after all.

As he dithered on which of the two to go with, Omrak saw the crooked, lightning-blasted tree that marked the location. He turned at the tree, spotting the tracks others who had come before him had made on the soft ground. Following it, he soon ascended the small hilltop where the ceremony was to be held. There, the bleating of sheep, tied carefully aside, mixed with the smell of burnt wood and opened caskets of mead.

"Omrak!" a voice called, one thick with the accent of home.

Omrak grinned, waving to the elderly man who presided over this event. The Feast of Winter's Coming was a familiar event that marked the marriage of Lund with Birgitta. They would sacrifice the sheep to Lund and then spend the evening drinking, roasting the sheep, and then offering the cooked meat to Birgitta. Those who did particularly well would receive a minor blessing from both Lund and Birgitta for the upcoming year of health and fertility, respectively.

The Feast itself was a minor ceremony, but after the long summer and fall preparations for winter, the Feast was one last event before the snow fell and blanketed the mountains. It was also, quite often, the time when those struggling with preparations might approach others for aid, when there was still time enough for a difference to be made in winter preparations.

And as Omrak gratefully received the horn of mead, it was a chance to drink and eat. Pushing aside adventuring worries for another day, Omrak focused on speaking with his countrymen and women, strangers one and all in this humid, overly warm, but ridiculously wealthy south.

Chapter 7

Unlike the Seven Stones, the Beaten Steel met the team in the Adventurer's Guild itself, in one of the many meeting rooms that could be rented. It was there that the party spoke with the Dwarf-led team leader, who was flanked by a Beastkin-lion and a human man. After introductions had been made, they'd launched into a quick summary of their organization and then a simple questioning of the team.

"Hrmmm . . . your Levels are low," Damun the Dwarf said.

"They are decent for only being Adventurers for just over two years now," Keck the human pointed out. "Not outstanding, but better than your average."

"We don't recruit average," Damun said.

"Well, of course, but we aren't," Daniel said.

Damun waved his hand, ignoring Daniel's interjection. He turned to the Lionkin, frowning at the still-silent man. Unlike most Beastkin in Brad, he had significantly more hair, including a riotous mane and a semi-beard, furred face. Still, he was much less bestial than Asin.

"Well, you going to say anything?" Damun said.

"I say no."

Damun frowned. "Why? They're not spectacular, but he's a healer. You don't need to be spectacular with a healer."

"They smell of trouble," the Lionkin replied.

"Shit. I guess that's that, then," Damun said, turning back to Daniel.

"What?" Daniel yelped. Omrak growled in surprise while Asin, surprisingly, looked perfectly calm. "That's it?"

"Yeah, sorry about that. If someone had spoken up earlier, we could all have been drinking," Damun said, already standing up.

"But . . . but . . ." Daniel stuttered, still surprised. After all the fawning he'd received, this was a surprise that he was trying to wrap his head around.

"Look, kid. You got a Beastkin scout too. The first lesson you learn—if your scout says no, you stop. Always listen to your scout," Damun said.

"But you're the leader," Omrak spoke up. "Should not your word hold greater weight?"

"Sure it does. But I'm the leader because I know when to listen. And if Chotu says you guys are trouble, you're trouble," Damun said. "And the Broken Steel doesn't look for trouble. We look for gold. We're a simple guild. We don't do politics; we don't do causes. We don't do trouble."

Having said his piece, the Dwarf strolled out, followed soon after by his teammates.

Daniel flopped back in his seat, staring up at the ceiling and muttering. "That was surprising."

"Still, maybe for the better. It seems they would not have wanted to offer you much aid," Omrak said.

"Yes," Asin said, then reached over and patted Daniel on shoulder in commiseration.

When the young man smiled at his friend, she grinned at him and added, "Breakfast?"

"We just ate!" Daniel protested, even as Omrak loudly agreed.

Shortly, Daniel found himself the only one seated as his friends enthusiastically left to eat a second breakfast since their initial meeting had gone so much faster.

At least, Daniel reflected, they had a second meeting to look forward to today.

***

Their second meeting took them deep into the nobles' quarters of Silverstone. In this case, it was further upstream and close to the river that bordered the city. Of course, while they used the water from the river for some of their purposes, mostly they pulled it from the central fountains that the Adventurers walked by, their contents drawn from hillside springs in the distance, dug deep and piped to the fountains at a gentle slope.

It was only because the flow itself was insufficient for the entire population that the river was in use at all, forcing the servants to draw upon it for more mundane tasks like cleaning and washing.

Strangely enough, the deeper they went into the quarters, the fewer city guards there were. It was only when Omrak brought the matter to the attention of the pair did he receive an answer.

"Personal guards," Daniel said, nodding to a pair standing outside the barred gates of a fenced-off mansion. "They keep the peace here. Since they are generally higher level, fewer Thieves and Pickpockets work the streets here. Those that do are circumspect on who and how often they target."

"Why?" Omrak said.

"Vengeful," Asin said, sniffing slightly. In the nobles' quarters, her bestial appearance received more than one disgusted glance. Several times Asin had to dodge aside when a carriage swerved a little too close to her or a pedestrian refused to move aside. Eventually, she either walked behind Omrak or in the centre of the group.

"Yes. They'll hire Investigators or Guard Captains or the like to find them," Daniel acknowledged.

He came to a stop in front of a high-walled enclosure, its contents within signified by the flapping flag that stood above the wall presenting a pair of entwined red roses in varying shades. Even with the minor wind that blew through the nobles' quarters, bringing with it the smell of the river and cool relief from the oppressive humidity, the flag flapped. A cheap but useless enchantment.

Which said a lot about the Guild itself, Daniel reflected. He turned his head sideways, noting that there were no guards standing outside or inside and hesitated on how to introduce themselves. No bell, either.

"Speak your business."

Daniel jumped, his left hand rising even as he pulled his mace from his inventory. A moment later as he hefted his weapon, did he realise he was not under attack.

"Speak your business."

Frowning, Daniel realised that the noise came from the stone pillars that held up the gates. He peered closer, realising that one particular stone was discolored in comparison to the rest, darker and with a faded silver-and-gold sigil on it.

"Speak your business."

"Magical door," Daniel said, shaking his head. But he replied to it, because, well, there was nothing to argue with. "We have an appointment with the guild. My name is Daniel Chai."

After speaking, Daniel remained still, staring at the stone. For long seconds, nothing happened. He frowned, straightening up and looking at his friends. He only received shrugs, making the healer frown. They waited in silence, Daniel frowning deeper and deeper before the doors finally swung open.

"I guess we go in?" he said.

The team shrugged, though Asin waved the healer ahead. He sniffed, pushed the doors apart wider as he kept walking. There was absolutely nothing to fear. Even if the ostentatious display of magic was rather . . . wasteful. He could not help but tot up the cost of both the enchantments, the doors that opened and closed by themselves, and the magical shielding that surrounded the guild hall. Only to find it staggering.

And excessive. To his surprise, within the compound there was not much wasted space for things like an ornamental lawn. Instead, the lawn—and the grounds leading up to the wall— had been converted into an archery range. It left the majority of the lawn itself untouched, with the archery butts set against the wall.

As for the hall, the guild had taken over the mansion that had once been there. Betraying its origins as the residence of a noble, fluted columns and high balconies overlooking the pristine grounds covered the building which was three times the size of the inn Daniel resided within. A large, double-doored entrance was open from which a single individual stood, awaiting the team as they walked across the gravel ground.

"Adventurer Chai. Adventurer Omrak. Adventurer Asin." The figure sketched a slight curtsy when they arrived before her. Flame-red hair, clad in a simple cream tunic and dark-brown vest ensemble, she presented a striking figure, especially in the tight leather pants. Both men blinked, covering their shock as the short-haired lady continued speaking. "The guildmaster is awaiting you."

"Thank you," Daniel said, taking a brief moment to clean his boots before following the lady as she turned and swept inside the stone-floored interior, one filled with multiple, woven wool and cloth wall hangings. As he caught up to her within, he spoke up. "I'm sorry, I missed your name."

"I did not give it," the woman replied with casual ease. "Eleanor Baumbridge. I am the guildmaster's assistant and party member."

"Oh, pleasure to meet you Adventurer Baumbridge," Daniel said. "And you can just call me Daniel."

"Very well." The woman strode ahead, down the carpeted corridor before stopping in front of one of many doorways, this one closed. Daniel had glimpsed from the various open doors a dining room, living rooms and even a pair of studies filled with numerous books and scrolls. This one, he assumed—correctly—when Eleanor swung the door open at a barked command from within, was an office.

The office itself was, like much of the building, richly appointed with drapes, tapestries and a well-woven carpet. A single wooden table, gleaming with oiled wood, dominated the room, while a series of chairs awaited their use. Seated at the table, caring for a pair of swords laid out before her, was the guildmaster.

"Guildmaster, your appointment," Eleanor said, striding within and taking a position at the side of the room next to a simple stand for refreshments.

Daniel stepped into the room, sketching a bow and stopping behind a chair. At the guildmaster's gesture, he took a seat, followed by his friends who had offered their own vocal or physical greetings in turn.

"My name is Alannah Pellegrino. I am the guildmaster of this branch of the Red Roses." She spoke easily, placing aside the oiled cloth she had been using. She glanced at her weapons for a second, verifying they were ready before beginning the process of putting them away. "I understand you are interested in joining us."

"Yes," Daniel replied. The other two chimed in their agreement as well.

"Why?" Alannah said, leaning forward. Pale green eyes flashed as she flicked her gaze over the three of them before settling on Daniel.

"Uhh . . . because we've been told—and experienced—that it's hard to improve and progress without the aid of a guild," Daniel said, speaking quickly.

"Is that the only reason?" Alannah said, her words cutting like the swords she sheathed.

Daniel flinched a little, at her gaze, at her words and the stark accusation. He hesitated on what to say, years of secrecy warring with the need to reveal something. Only to have a tail smack him in the back on his butt, as Asin spoke.

"What know?" Asin said, emerald eyes gleaming.

Alannah's gaze flicked over to the Catkin, her gaze growing considering. She turned back to Daniel, sniffing a little as he kept silent at Asin's not-so-subtle signal. Eventually, she broke the silence, as Omrak knew better than to butt in. "We made enquiries. When an Adventurer who previously refused our overtures then suddenly begins contacting guilds, it often signals trouble."

Daniel grunted. Of course. Regret flashed through him, as he realised perhaps he could have gotten a better deal, prepared better. Foolish. The hope of being an Adventurer, just another person, had never been but a foolish dream. His Gift—his curse—had always meant his life would be dictated by it. Just like any of the other Gifted.

"Learn?" Asin said, her voice rising at the end as ears swivelled forward in curiosity.

Rather than answer directly, Alannah turned her head to regard Elanor. The aide blinked, then spoke up. "In some ways, nothing of great import. Until, of course, we learnt of your time with the Three Skills. And then we inquired further."

Daniel frowned.

"Something to understand. Nothing that is known by one noble house will ever truly be secret," Eleanor said. She smiled grimly. "Including the fact that you are one of the Gifted." Daniel deflated, his head hanging low as Eleanor continued. "Unlike the Three Skills, we do have contacts within this city. And Karlak. It took us a little while, but we were able to put together the picture of what happened with regard to the Champion."

Daniel let out a huff, shrinking a little into himself at the last sentence. He knew he should not have. For a moment he wondered if the Champion had betrayed him, then realised it might just have been any one of the dozen who had seen his condition.

"I ask again. Why do you want to join us?" Alannah said, her voice biting.

"I . . ." Daniel paused, then raised his head, meeting her gaze. "I need allies. For when word of my Gift reaches higher."

"What do you fear?"

"Being forced to be nothing more than a Healer. Being forced to use my Gift, exhaustively," Daniel said.

"Your Price." Alannah's tone brooked no argument.

"Yes."

Silence met his brief answer, even Asin and Omrak looking over to Daniel curiously.

Drawing a deep breath, Daniel spoke of his old pain, his old hurt. The tragedy of his Gift, the burden he carried. "My memories."

"What?!" Eleanor yelped. "That . . . but you . . ."

She was not the only one as the others all exclaimed, looking surprised. Looking worried.

"I don't use it much. And sometimes, the memories don't . . . matter. When I'm eating, when I'm bathing . . ." Daniel hastily said to his friends. "And the amount varies. For small things, I don't ever notice it."

"But some are important," Alannah said, her voice still cold and flat. Of them all, she was the one who had reacted least. "And yet, you still wield it."

"Yes," Daniel said, meeting her cold gaze. "Does it matter?"

"It does. A Gifted who refuses to pay the Price of his Gift is of no use," Alannah said. "They could be just a normal recruit then."

Daniel nodded in understanding. He looked around, his gaze falling on the refreshment table and found himself pointing to it. "May I?"

A nod, and a short break later, the group all had cups of watered wine in hand. When they were all settled, Alannah continued her questioning. "Now, tell me. How powerful is your Gift?"

"Don't you know already?" Daniel looked pointedly at Eleanor.

"I want to hear it from you, directly," Alannah said. She leaned forward, hands clasping around the cup on her desk. "And I resent the waste of my time. You are coming to us with your appeal. You can choose to answer our questions fully. Or you can leave."

Asin stirred, while Daniel flushed in anger. Omrak growled a little, hand clenching around his cup. "Daniel's Gift is powerful! It can heal anything. You'd be lucky to acquire him."

A single interrogative eyebrow had Daniel answering, reluctantly. "Not everything, but close to it. I can . . . sense the damage and changes in a body and fix it."

"Old wounds?" A nod. "Tumors?" Another nod. "Maladies of the mind?"

Daniel hesitated at that. "It . . . depends."

"On?" Alannah said.

"On the extent and kind of damage. I can sometimes, if it's new enough, fix the problems. Maybe even head off the onset of damage. Sometimes it's simple. Other times it repeats," Daniel said. "A lot of it is . . . self-inflicted?" He frowned, unsure of how to explain it.

"Interesting." Alannah said, tapping her lips.

From her spot against the wall, Eleanor spoke up. "We'd want to keep that quiet anyway."

"Why?" Asin asked.

The Catkin spoke up curiously. Interestingly, Daniel observed, she kept her focus on Eleanor mostly, rather than the guildmaster.

"If his Gift works like most, the more extensive the healing, the more memories he loses," Eleanor said, receiving a confirming nod from Daniel. "Repairing mental ailments—of any kind—will open the Adventurer up to significant requests from some of our members."

"Lutz-cursed dungeon-fear?" Omrak said, naming an ailment that many faced after years of delving Dungeons. Or some particularly bad close encounters. The effects were wide ranging from flashbacks, insomnia and night sweats, irrational outbursts of emotions, depression, and more. Sadly, while normal healers and healing potions could fix the physical ailments, mental ones were much more difficult. Even a priest found it difficult, though they at least had a better track record.

"That, though there are known remedies. But for old age? The forgetfulness and dementia some of the heads of noble houses get?" Eleanor shook her head. "No. Better not to begin."

"The royals . . ." Alannah said.

"Would have to be told. But they are different," Eleanor said. Her smile twisted slightly. "As they are in most things."

There were some firm nods, since that was a rather obvious comment.

"So powerful, significantly more so than most healing spells." Seeing something on Daniel's face, Alannah frowned. "More powerful than even a **Full Regeneration**?"

"I believe so, if I was intent on it," Daniel said. "What I have learnt of the spell's limitations indicate that my Gift can do more with less."

"Less?" A raised eyebrow.

"Less material. A lower overall cost in . . ." Daniel gestured vaguely to his head.

"Memory. Fascinating. But your ability to use your Gift instead of Mana increases your versatility by far," Alannah said, nodding. "Why do you not spend more time exploring your Gift, building upon your healing abilities? Surely this Gift of yours would allow you to progress quickly. Even with your focus split, you are a decent healer from what I understand."

Daniel's lips tightened, before he finally answered when Alannah was content to stay silent. "I want to be an Adventurer. It's what I've always wanted."

"And so, instead of doing what the Goddess has obviously planned for you, you choose to indulge in your own whims." The Guild Leader's voice was flat, neither friendly nor accusatory.

"I work the hospices whenever I can," Daniel replied defensively. "I help more people there than most healers do who work regularly."

"Mmm, and you could do so much more with your Gift if you studied further. With your Mana, your spells could be much more powerful," Eleanor said. "If you didn't split your focus, you could specialise your spells further."

"I . . ."

"Hero Daniel does not need to explain his choices to you," Omrak rumbled. "He does good work, as an Adventurer and healer. The subjugation of Dungeons is important."

"Which anyone can do," Alannah said. "We have new Adventurers arriving in the city every day. Any individual with a strong arm and a willing heart can be an Adventurer. Few are offered Gifts."

"I wasn't offered it," Daniel said bitterly. "It was just something I was born with."

"Nonetheless." Alannah said.

"Arrogant."

The single word by Asin had the group turn to the Catkin, who released a deep sniff of disapproval.

When she was certain they were listening, she added, "Erlis chose. But future uncertain."

"We should, however, attempt to divine her wishes," Alannah said, "or we scorn the very gifts that she offers us."

"Arrogant," Asin restated.

Alannah's eyes narrowed as she stared at the Catkin, and in the growing brittle silence, Daniel spoke up. "I answered your questions. Perhaps you can answer mine. Will you take us, knowing what you do now? And if so, what would you offer?"

Alannah frowned, considering. "We will. As for our offer . . ." She shook her head. "That will have to be re-evaluated."

"Oh." Daniel fell silent. "How fast before you make a decision?"

"Not me," Alannah said, shaking her head. "Such a decision will be handled by those above me. They will decide such matters."

"Above you?" Daniel said, surprised.

"Yes. You ask us to intervene between you and the nobility and royalty. What we'll do and how far we'll go, and what we will offer will be handled by the true master of the guild."

Daniel numbly nodded at last, understanding her point. It was not what he wanted, but it was, perhaps, the best that she could offer. In truth, he had to admit, it was likely that she would not be the first to speak to those above her.

The more his Gift was revealed, the higher the stakes became.

Chapter 8

Daniel yawned, though he happily took the wrapped greased paper sandwiches that Asin handed him. He stored them away in his inventory, there being enough space at the outset of the delve. Later on, if they managed to find enough loot, his inventory might run short— though he doubted that would happen in this delve—but for now, it was simpler to store it away. Less likelihood of his lunch getting squashed or otherwise damaged.

Of course, Daniel eyed the group gathering a short distance from the entrance to Porthos. Omrak was smiling, already happily chatting with Zef, one of the many new members of the Seven Stone guilds that were supposed to watch this delve.

Beside the scaled drake and Northerner, Lady Nyssa the sonic Mage lounged, hiding a yawn behind her hand. She was dressed in expensive, form-fitting dark red leathers that were suppled and glowed with hints of Mana and enchantments. Nearby, Harlow was attempting and failing to engage the Mage in a conversation. He was wearing a simple set of padded leather armor with a sheathed short sword on one side and a small handheld crossbow strapped to his back with a stack of bolts attached just above the belt.

A short distance away, Anne the archer stood by herself, fussily going over a pack of medicinal and herbal ingredients. It was a simple first aid kit that Daniel was very familiar with, though he spotted a few unusual changes. As much as magic made sense, often simple herbal tinctures and pastes could be used for non-major injuries like sprained wrists and torn ligaments.

As the seventh bell rang, a final figure strode out of the side street. A towering bear of a man, he had a large shield slung over his shoulder and carried a large warhammer with a spike on the other end. Unlike Daniel's own mace, his warhammer's shaft was nearly five feet long by itself and heavy enough to make Daniel's arm throb in imagined sympathy.

The newcomer flicked his gaze over the group, then stuck his hand out to Daniel. "Party Leader Dockery. Blue corded, Advanced Adventurer. I'll be taking this party in. I understand you'll be coming with us but watching only?"

Daniel introduced himself and his friends quickly before answering the question with an affirmative. "We'll hang back and watch, if you don't mind."

"That's fair. We'll be taking a diamond formation and treat you as an unaffiliated party in that case," Dockery said. "That means watch yourself, too."

"Of course," Daniel acknowledged.

Content with what had been said, Dockery turned to the group and barked out orders to the unpartied members. He quickly assigned their roles. Harlow was scouting ahead, Zef behind and followed by Anne and Lady Nyssa. He himself would take the rear position, acting as rearguard and emergency aid.

It was, Daniel had to admit, a relatively standard party formation. With enough space, the two long-range damage dealers could fire their arrows and magic to aid the team while Zef held off attackers with his spear, allowing Harlow to fall back to the group and remove any stragglers. If necessary, the team could also rush forward to aid Harlow if he was caught in a surprise attack.

Daniel's own team took a somewhat similar approach with Asin ranging ahead, Omrak behind, and himself at the back. Of course, he was a poor ranged attacker, more suited to close combat—a long-time concern for their team.

"If we're done?" Dockery said, bringing Daniel's attention back to him. Receiving a nod, he led them all down to the first level of the Dungeon.

***

Floating landbridges that moved, clouds beneath and above their feet, and an ever-changing map were all characteristics of the first level for Porthos. It was a level that the team were well familiar with, having trekked and attempted it multiple times. Ever since the loss of their other team members though, the trio had given up on Porthos due to their incompatibility with the monsters within.

"Six behind!" Daniel shouted, leveling the rockbow and aiming at the swooping group of attackers.

He held his fire though, waiting for the monsters to arrive at the optimal range for his modified crossbow. The rockbow slung explosive rocks which shattered under great stress—like being fired from a nocked crossbow-sling at high speeds—and pelted monsters with the shards. The shards themselves did little damage, except to the tender and delicate webbed wings of the monsters attacking them.

Six flying, red-skinned Imps with bat-like wings and long, black grasping claws flew at Daniel as he hunched down, calming his breath. At the right moment, he triggered the attack, watching the rock fly out and explode, catching three of the creatures. One was hit and another spiralled away as they flinched from the attack, the lead Imp taking the attack in the face and clawing at its eyes. The last, its wings shredded, fell past the group, off into the depths of the dungeon.

Before Daniel could ready another attacker, Omrak stepped forward and swung his weapon, bisecting an Imp and warding off the attentions of the other two. As they winged away, one fell as Asin's thrown knife caught it in the back, taking her weapon with it.

Asin let out a snarled curse, watching her throwing knife disappear—along with the Imp's Mana stone—before she turned back to scanning for additional dangers. Daniel worked the sling and bow of his rockbow, turning slightly so he could regard the team ahead of them. They were, for the most part, only receiving the stragglers of the swarm that had formed around the Seven Stones team's attackers.

Watching the group, Daniel could not help but admit they were good. Even thrown together as they were—with only a few of the team members having worked together before, as they'd confirmed over a snack an hour before—they still worked together well. There were occasional hiccups, moments where the group expected another to take over, but for the most part, they knew their roles and did them well.

Scouting ahead, Harlow had fallen further away from the main body of the team and was loosing attacks from his crossbow. To Daniel's surprise, the wrist bow—a small, one-handed crossbow that could be easily strung and fired one-handed—was an enchanted weapon. Bolts released from the weapon turned into flaming attacks. Of course, the Imps were immune to the fire, but it mattered little when each individual Imp was skewered and sent into the sky.

Standing close to the Mage and archer, Zef had his spear out, waving it around to ward off the Imps. He'd cast it away at the start of the encounter before recalling the weapon, managing to skewer one Imp to start and another on the return. Now, he kept to his task of guarding the group while the two members of the team with long-range weapons went to work.

Anne, the archer, did the majority of the work, using **Splitting Arrows** to carve large furrows into the Imp swarm, while Lady Nyssa was much more conservative on her use of magic. Like any Mana user, she had to be careful about the spells she used because of the low regeneration of Mana. However, being rich and a noble, the woman had found a method to work around that by leaking a little magic into the enchanted leather gear, using the modified armor to channel and boost her attacks. In this way, she could sustain specialised attacks at a higher level, unleashing **Sonic Cones** at the Imps without bottoming out.

From Daniel's knowledge, such enchantments were incredibly expensive—much more than the dozens of gold the enchantments he and his team purchased and were, instead, in the tens of hundreds of gold coin level. It was due to the level of Mastery an enchanter required in Mana control and the need for rare enscribing materials. Even if one had the money, it was often impossible to have such an enchantment made, as all the work had to be customised. Worse, once she out-leveled the enchantment, it would no longer work, and the entire work would have to be scrapped.

Expensive, wasteful in many ways, but perfectly encapsulating the advantage the nobles had in Brad.

"Daniel!" A shouted roar from Omrak made Daniel turn away to focus on the next group of

Imps to dive off the edge of a floating island. He raised the rockbow to his shoulder, pushing aside the moment of jealousy.

At least the Seven Stones trained their people well. Thus far, at least. They'd have to see what they did when they made their way deeper.

***

Fourth floor. Deeper than the team had ever gone before in Porthos. After all, they'd done Artos as a group, but before they could do more, they'd had to leave on their expedition. Once they came back, they needed to rework their team mechanics without their archer. And then they'd moved down the floors, only to have Rob, their Enchanter, leave for a better offer. Leaving just the three of them, once more.

In many ways, Daniel was grateful that his friends had not left. Asin was a talented scout and had an open invitation to join the Broken Chains Guild. Omrak had fewer choices since he was a typical frontline fighter. Even so, few parties would turn down a front-line fighter with a taunt proficiency that they were willing to use. Too many grew scared, afraid of the pain and the danger.

Then again, Daniel remembered Omrak before they met. Constantly bloody, constantly injured, and poor as he bought healing potions to deal with the injuries. Perhaps his choice to stay was more practical. Daniel dismissed the thought soon after. With someone else, someone less straightforward than the blond Adventurer, Daniel might believe that.

Not with Omrak.

And thus, they were here. Fourth floor, new section of Porthos. Rather than floating stone walkways and swarms of Imps, they stood on a beach, an aqua green ocean rolling in, waves pounding against the surf. They moved along the beach, one eye on the water and the other on the sand dunes that dotted the beach.

Rising from the sand dunes were monsters. Giant Crabs, their shells made of steel and bronze, their pincers lunging forward to crush bone and armor. Sand fleas the size of dogs that burrowed out from the ground and leapt at the group. Thankfully, they didn't attack in groups, but at random—when whim and hunger drove them to it. Sometimes, this occurred in the middle of the battle. Other times, when the group had passed what seemed to be a perfectly normal stretch of land.

Even so, the Seven Stones team took it all on without an issue. Zef's spear, glowing with the powered **Skill Proficiency** he offered it, punched forward through gaps in armor, skewering crabs and fleas alike. Lady Nyssa's sonic bolts drove the crabs insane, offering a painful distraction that allowed Harlow or Anne to drive their attacks in. Even Dockery took part, using his powerful hammer to crack open shells to end the monsters.

As for Daniel's team, Omrak found a much simpler method of dealing with the occasional crab that threatened them. Bare-handed, he'd duck in close, gripping one side of the monster and heaving upwards, tossing it over. Giant monster or not, when it was on its back, it was a simple matter for him or Daniel to end the fight.

All went swimmingly, until the Floor Boss arrived—a monster twice the size of the oversized Giant Crabs, twice as tall as Omrak and nearly four times as wide. It held itself off the ground on thin legs, moving forward and snapping its pincers.

The Seven Stones team pivoted immediately, Dockery barking orders. Zef imbued his first attack, throwing his spear as hard as he could and watching it glance off the metal carapace of the Floor Boss. On the other hand, Anne skittered backwards, an arrow drawn to her cheek as she poured Mana and Stamina into the attack. It was a mixed **Skill Proficiency**, one requiring both

Mana and Stamina and significant build-up time, but was all the more powerful because of that.

Even as Zef recalled his weapon, Harlow was sprinting around the crab, attempting to get behind it. He stayed far away from the legs, knowing how fast the crab could scuttle to the side if it chose to. Rather than risk that, or fire his ineffective fire bolts, he sought an opening. At the side, Lady Nyssa kept throwing small **Sonic Cones** at the creature, focusing her attacks on its shell, attempting to resonate the shell and crack it. Angered by the attacks, the crab charged the Mage, only to be blocked by Zef's returning spear. Just behind Zef, Dockery stood, watchful for danger.

"Do you think they need help?" Daniel asked, as he shifted the grip on his warhammer. A part of him wanted to get a strike in anyway, just to see if he could capture the monster.

"Ask," Asin said.

"Aye, they will ask when they need it," Omrak said. "Though I dearly do wish to test myself against that Boss."

The pair beside him could only nod in agreement. They stood aside, watching as the team from Seven Stones took the Floor Boss apart, its shell shattering as it wobbled further and further before being struck by the **Empowered Arrow**. In the gap, while its pincer was grasping the spear from Zef, Harlow jumped, plunging his short sword deep into its body, twisting it around and around as he rode the monster to its death. Only once did Dockery step in, and that to help finish off the already dying monster.

"I'd say they're pretty damn good, don't you?" Daniel muttered, shaking his head. The three of them could win against the Floor Boss. But it would have taken them time. And blood. Neither of which they would have cared to shed.

Chapter 9

Five floors, two Floor Bosses, and one mild but debilitating injury later, the Seven Stones Guild had exited. As a favor, Daniel had cast a simple **Healer's Mark** to allow Lady Nyssa to recover from the twisted ankle faster, ensuring she could return to training the next day. After the team had passed on their farewells to one another, they had parted ways, with Daniel and friends travelling to the Adventurers Guild to sell the few Mana stones they had acquired.

While seated at the tavern's dining table, snacking on a plate of deep-fried pork skin—made from some magical wild boar that were raised within the city limits he had been assured—that they were interrupted. Mattias Gill strolled over to their table, leaning on the table slightly as he stared at Daniel, ignoring the other two Adventurers. "I am very disappointed in you, Healer."

"Huh?" was all that Daniel could think to say to that sudden pronouncement.

"I thought we had an understanding. And here you are, going to so many others, speaking to them about things that you should not." Mattias shook his head. "One wonders if you ever truly wanted to hide your Gift."

Daniel twitched at the pronouncement, though the general hubbub in the Guild was sufficient to drown out Mattias's words. No one looked over, no one checked on the Adventurer or wondered what Gift he spoke of.

"And who might you be, Hero?" Omrak rumbled from the side, the blond Adventurer sitting straight in his chair in an attempt at intimidation.

Mattias flashed a quick look at Omrak, muttering "Be quiet, child" before he turned back to Daniel. "I'm very disappointed in you. We were kind enough to give you time to think, to consider. And here you are, telling others about what we learnt. So consider our initial offer withdrawn." Daniel nodded, opening his mouth to remark only to be cut-off. "Instead, you'll join us, alone."

"That sounds like a demand," Daniel said, frowning.

"It is a statement." Mattias leaned over, his voice dropping. "You do not want to disappoint me a second time. The Three Skills do not like being crossed. Nor will my sponsors be willing to take your reluctance well."

"And that's a threat," Daniel added. His lips pursed even further even as Asin edged back a little from the table, clearing the distance to her daggers.

"From me? No. Just a warning." Mattias straightened. "My sponsors will not allow you to take your Gifts to another."

"I think we're done here," Daniel said, his anger flaring at the threats.

"Fool." Mattias spat to the side. The altercation between the group was drawing attention though, so he just turned and walked away, leaving the trio to stare at his fading back.

"Well, that was . . . different," Daniel said, shaking his head. Very few people would be willing to threaten a healer. There were ways of course, but being so blatant seemed strange to him.

"I do not think you should join them," Omrak said.

"Yes," Asin added, simply.

"Agreed. But I don't like those threats. Do you think we should inform the Guild?" Daniel said, absently smiling and nodding in reassurance to the few Adventurers who were still looking at them.

"Yes." Asin flicked her gaze to the backrooms and the staircase leading up to where the guildmaster would be.

"Ah hell . . ." Daniel said.

It was best to report it, just in case. Still, he was certain it was going to raise numerous questions that he had no real desire to answer. And, in truth, there was little the guildmaster could do for verbal threats other than note it.

Without evidence, they could only be more watchful.

Still, it worried Daniel and his friends. Theirs was a dangerous profession as it stood, and all too often Adventurers did not return from the Dungeon for entirely practical reasons. A single mistake, pushing oneself too hard, greed, and just bad luck could end an Adventuring team as much as malfeasance.

Standing up, Daniel headed for the back offices, followed closely along by his friends. It was best to get this done.

***

As expected, there was little that the Guild could do for them but note the entire incident. In fact, they had not even managed to see the guildmaster themselves, instead speaking to one of his many assistants who wrote down the entire incident, promising to inform the guards to keep an eye out for threats.

It was such that the next morning, the trio met up again before the Guild Hall in a rather glum mood. As Daniel walked over, he noted that Asin was speaking with a team of Beastkin, a group of six Adventurers. Two were Foxkin, squat and fast with the red fur of their clans. One had Foxkin fur; the other had fur on the rear of his hands and running down the back of his neck and sported a strange mutton chop beard. The front-line fighters were a Bearkin and Boarkin, wielding a greatsword and halberd respectively. As for the other two, they were both Birdkin, though Daniel was uncertain of their type. Rather than hair, they had short feathers that seemed at first glance to be hair. The fact that they both carried bows indicated they were the long-range support.

"Daniel!" Asin called out to the healer. She waved him over and then tilted her head to the Bearkin, letting out a low growl in the Beastkin language to the others.

"Ah, Asin wishes us to greet you directly," the Bearkin said. "I am Wasme. This is Kord" — a nod to the Boarkin— "These two brothers are Pol and Mol" —a glance to the Foxkin— "and the sisters are Ash and Oak" —for the final Birdkin.

Daniel greeted the group, and then watched as the introductions were repeated when Omrak arrived as well. Looking the group over, he spotted a guild badge that they all wore, a simple chain that had been shattered in the center.

"I'm assuming there's a reason for a party from the Broken Chain to be meeting us here? Or is this really just a coincidence?" Daniel said.

"Not coincidence," Asin said, her tail lashing out behind her lazily. "Show."

"Show . . . never mind," Daniel said. He got it. Team mechanics. "Don't you think we should have had a discussion beforehand. About what you can offer?"

"Unnecessary. We know enough about you. But we're Beastkin. The Broken Chain is our largest Guild; we are but half as strong as the five," Wasme said. "What you see is what we can provide. Companionship, training."

"And you want to show us what kind of training you can provide," Daniel said, finishing off the unspoken thought.

"Yes. If you will allow us."

Daniel looked over at Omrak who shrugged. He looked a little unhappy since they had planned to enter the Dungeon themselves today to earn some coin. While they had made some profit from the Mana stones they had picked up, Porthos was just not a great Dungeon for them, even when they were not purposely holding back. Still, it was but one more day, and they could enter again tomorrow.

As for Asin, Daniel knew he did not need to ask. After all, she had been the one to arrange this.

"All right, let's see what the Broken Chain can do." Daniel offered his hand again which Wasme clasped with one and then slapped

Daniel's shoulder with the other. The stout Adventurer found himself nearly knocked off his feet by the Bearkin, a part of him noting the carefully-leashed strength held within the bulky muscles of the Bearkin.

"Just give me a second while I get a rockbow. Wasn't really thinking we'd be going to Porthos again . . ." Daniel said.

***

Two floors down, the group were having a short lunch break on one of the many floating islands that made up this floor. The second floor of Porthos was similar to the first in all but volume and the addition of the occasional moving walkway trap. As the group rested, the Birdkin kept watch, bow idly held in one hand while they tore into strips of jerky in the other.

"What do you think?" Kord, the Boarkin, asked. He was using a spatula to spoon mouthfuls of yellow rice, vegetables, and strips of meat into his mouth with gusto, the tiny tusks that rose from his lips easily avoided from long years of practise. "We're different, aren't we?"

"Very much so, Hero Kord," Omrak rumbled. "You and Hero Wasme are strong, and the Bear's roars drive the Imps away so easily."

"Beastkin traits," Kord said, grinning. "We can buy **Blood Skills** if we wish, beyond just normal skills. Wasme uses **Territory Roar** for the fear effect. Mine's more focused on getting them to fight me."

"So I noticed," Omrak said. "I have a similar skill too."

"Northerner?" At Omrak's nod, he chuckled. "Does it ever strike you as strange that the only people who don't have special bloodline **Skill Proficiencies** are the humans of Brad and the surroundings?"

"They did," one of the Foxkin interrupted. Daniel glanced at him, trying to remember if it was Pol or Mol. Their names were so similar that he kept getting them mixed up. "Father said that they lost it because they angered Erlis."

"Bah! Father says a lot of things when he's deep in the joosh. Anyway, Priest Leow said it was because they diluted their blood too much. And that's why we shouldn't dilute ours further either."

Daniel could not help but smile slightly at the bickering pair of brothers. In truth, in terms of the Northerners he was not certain there was any blood-related reason why they had different Skill Proficiencies they could choose. Certainly, unlike the Beastkin, he felt no difference when he worked on their bodies. Beastkin on the other hand—those were a pain and a half to handle.

"Not true. Knights and Lords." Asin spoke up, raising a hand and counting off. "Nobles."

"Yes, but those are . . . well, bloodline related. But I do hear that it's not a common title in other countries," Kord said, rubbing his chin. "The Republic of Sift comes to mind."

"Bah! It's not much of a republic, being a single city and a few towns," Wasme said, coming over to sit down. "More like a big province."

"You're all very well-informed," Daniel said, his voice tinged with surprise.

Few people bothered to learn much about other countries. As it was, few individuals would bother leaving their own hometown, never mind going so far as to travel to another city or town over. Adventurers were obviously different, with their need to go where Dungeons were, but even then, few needed to concern themselves about countries outside of their own.

"Beastkin hobby," Wasme said, heavy brows drawing down in a frown. "We talk about other countries, hoping to find one that desires us. Or how they treat others of our kind. Always good to have an ear to the wind."

There were nods from all around, making Daniel wince internally. The continued persecution of the once-enslaved race was a sore point, for humans and Beastkin alike.

"But enough of that. Kord was speaking of our training methods. And it is different. Between our bloodline abilities and our greater flexibility in terms of physical skills, we have learned to make do without Mages and their flexibility," Wasme said. "Our frontline fighters are stronger than most, being made up of Beastkin of the appropriate blood." He paused and grinned. "Mostly."

"Mostly." Asin echoed, her grin widening.

"Mostly?" Omrak echoed.

"There are the stubborn. The unusual," Wasme said, gesturing towards the pair of Foxkin. "Some grow larger than normal. Others are just more suited to it by temperament. Not everything is a matter of blood. Though much is, for us."

There were nods again from the Beastkin before Pol piped up. "But you're still going to find it better to guess based off a 'Kin's animal than not."

Mol added, "And outside of the Guild, you'll find fewer deviants. Both civilian and in other Guilds."

"That's right. They just aren't as accepting as we are." Pol grinned.

Wasme just shook his head, his voice rumbling as he continued. "But we do like healers. Those are always helpful. Even if we have fewer than we like."

"I don't think there's a Guild that has as many as they'd like," Daniel said.

"Maybe not, but Beastkin healers are even more precious. Few who are competent would enter a Dungeon. And few human healers are willing to study our bodies well enough not to cause inadvertent harm," Wasme said.

Daniel grimaced, nodding at that. Initially, when he healed Asin of anything complicated, he often had to tap into his Gift to understand her body. By now, of course, he knew it well enough;

but with the sheer variety of Beastkin, it would be something he would need to do frequently. Even if he saw Beastkin in the hospice too and was learning there, there was a difference between knowing and understanding.

"I—we—like what we see," Daniel said, glancing at Omrak and Asin to get confirming nods. "But there's more than just tactics that we have to be concerned about."

"Yes, I unde—" Wasme was interrupted by a shrill hoot.

He turned, frowning to the Birdkin guard who had made the noise, only for her to point at an approaching party on one of the land bridges.

Automatically, the group shifted, eyeing the new team. Daniel noted how they grew tenser, how they moved apart slightly. More than one of the Beastkin checked the location of their weapons, made sure they were loose in their sheaths. It was a level of caution that Daniel frowned at before he remembered last night's threat. Sharing a look with his own team, he checked his own equipment.

In short order, the new team had managed to make their way over to the group. The leader, a scruffy-looking human with her hair tied up in a high ponytail, smiled as she walked over. But she had her hands resting on the paired short swords on her hips, and the team split apart the moment they had space. Perhaps it was automatic—long lessons learnt from delving—or it could be something else, but from Asin's straight tail, Daniel was leaning towards the second.

"Hail, fellow Adventurers. You don't mind sharing this island, do you? We're a little beat after our last encounter." In contrast to her words, the group looked entirely untouched and quite energetic.

Wasme smiled, walking over to her, his sword still slung over his shoulder. "Actually, it's a pretty small island. Perhaps you could move on?"

"Come now, there's no need to be so unfriendly." The raven-haired woman continued to speak as she closed the distance.

"'Ware," Ash said, drawing and raising her bow in one fluid motion. Her sister mimed her actions, taking another target as she moved to flank the group further.

"Rude. But what can you expect of beasts?" the woman muttered. She smiled brightly, eyes tracking over the Beastkin and Daniel's party to stop on him finally before she laughed. "I guess we do this the hard way."

The next moment, the new team threw themselves into action, weapons coming out of their sheaths, and chaos emerged.

***

Asin shrunk down for the first major action the new team took was to engage a spell. It shrouded the entire floating island in darkness, making the arrows that Ash and Oak fired go off course a little. Asin could hear the chime of metal arrowhead and blade echoing in the heavy, cloying darkness as the enemy team leader engaged **Flawless Parry**. However, the second arrow had a softer, more muted and squelchy end, burying itself within the body of the second in command. Of course, that individual was the tank, so it would likely only slow him down a little, but any damage was better than none.

The darkness that wrapped them initially was all-encompassing, forcing Asin to scurry—carefully—along the ground with care. But already, the pupils in her eyes were widening, drinking in the light that crept through the spell. Vague outlines began to form before her, the enemy team already splitting apart and aiming for the other Beastkin. Behind her, Asin could hear Omrak and Daniel cursing, falling into a defensive formation back-to-back.

She nodded to herself, grateful her friends were smart. They did not have the advantages the Beastkin did. Better for them to take care of themselves first. Oak and Ash were moving closer too, storing their bows and pulling out short swords and daggers. As Sparrowkin, they had good eyesight and fast reflexes, but none of the other enhanced senses. In the darkness, they were just as vulnerable.

A roar from Kord yanked her attention to him for a second. Already a pair of the enemy team members had been headed to him, but now a crossbow bolt buried itself in his body, meant initially for Pol. The Boarkin had begun glowing, triggering a rage ability much like Omrak's.

And then, finally reaching the point in the island she had been aiming for; Asin threw her first knife of the battle. It was a simple attack, one that blossomed into multiple throwing knives that harried the pair of attackers closing in on Kord. **Fan of Knives** combined with her lightning enchantment dug into human skin, shocking and distracting the pair.

The leader was not among them, engaged as she was with Wasme. Flickers of movement, as the greatsword-wielding bear attempted to strike the faster, wilier opponent. Already, he bled freely from multiple surface cuts. The woman was fast and gifted, outfighting and out-maneuvering the half-blind Bearkin. He did not have the night sight that she did, though his expanded senses let him gauge roughly where his opponent was. Giant sweeps with his big weapon were a danger as well, forcing his opponent to focus on him rather than leaving for the greater threat. The threat of Pol and Mol brought to bear as they fell on their opponents' backline.

The pair of Foxkin had night vision just like her, nocturnal predators whose eyes worked just as well in low light. Expanded senses, greater agility and an innate cunning had them slipping from the darkness to pounce on the archer and the Mage. Short swords flashed, cutting into bodies, and screams erupted from the enemy team.

Broken from the unnatural draw of Kord's **Primal Challenge,** one of his opponents spun away. Only to be hit in the side as the Boarkin triggered another of his blood abilities—**Ferocious Charge**—and knocked his distracted opponent off the island itself. His long, drawn-out scream of surprise was muted due to the spell, legs and hands flapping in the air as he dropped.

But the attack had come at cost, allowing Kord's other opponent to drive a sword into his side. The Boarkin staggered for a second, eyes wide, before his rage ability drew him back to his feet. Asin howled, having just finished tossing a knife at the enemy leader as she spotted the attack from the corner of her eyes. Even as she ran forward, Kord started to turn around, only for his opponent to yank his sword out sideways, bisecting the spine and dropping the Boarkin to the floor.

Asin snarled in rage, tail lashing out behind her, the gravel stone beneath her bare feet suddenly making it much harder for her to reach Kord's enemy. She watched him fall before she launched herself into the air. Faster than she could have believed possible if she had not seen, felt, it herself, the swordsman had whipped his sword out and lunged at her flying body. All she could do was twist her body slightly as she was about to be skewered.

Only for the attack to be pushed off-line, tearing a line of pain along her side as the unnaturally sharp sword cut through leather. Her enchanted defensive necklace had forced the sword aside as it impacted her hardened aura. Then she was on him, legs and body smashing into him, knife driving deep into the gap between neck and shoulder pauldrons. Her electrified aura arced as it came into contact with the swordsman, and even as he attempted to push her off, pommel striking her, she held on. One knife lodged deep in his chest, the other stabbing again and again as it attempted to drive through chainmail in his side.

Her struggle narrowed for long seconds, long minutes as her opponent struggled to survive her onslaught. Eventually, he stopped moving entirely and Asin looked up, taking in the fight again. Wasme was still standing, though he was bleeding heavily. Kord was on the ground, unmoving, while Pol was missing. Among the corpses of the other three Adventurers, Mol stood, crying. The only individual left in the slowly fading darkness was the team leader, who had backed off from Wasme and was now surrounded by her own team and the Bearkin.

"Why did you attack us?" Wasme snarled, tears in the big bear's eyes.

"Damn. Easy targets they said. Just beasts, they said," the dual-wielding woman muttered to herself, turning from side-to-side as she ignored Wasme. "I knew it was too good to be true."

"Surrender, tell us why you did this, and we'll let you live," Daniel said, his shield held up in front of himself defensively.

"Har! Do you see their eyes? The anger they show. The beasts will never let me off." She laughed, clashing her swords together. "So you might as well get this over with."

"Who hired you?" Wasme growled again.

"Ask the healer." And then, while the group was still startled, she dashed out from the enclosed ring, picking a space between the two greatsword-wielding fighters. Their reflexive swings missed and clipped her gently, leaving a trail of blood before she escaped.

Directly into the pair of Birdkin, who stabbed forwards in unison with their blades. To their surprise, rather than block the attacks, the woman sheathed her blades in their bodies, taking the attack herself. Pinned in her chest and shoulder, she still tried to twist the short sword in Oak's body, Ash having managed to rip the weapon away from her own side.

And then Asin was there, hacking down with her knife. She cut off the woman's hand, leaving the weapon inside Oak as she booted the crazed woman away. Too slow. Again. But Daniel was moving too, dashing over to begin casting, to fix what he could. Magic formed in his hand, Minor Healing already materializing as he got ready to fix the damage done to Oak.

A healer, a compassionate human. And perhaps, the cause of all this tragedy.

Chapter 10

It was a much more subdued group that exited the Dungeon later that afternoon. Even injured and with party members lost, they still had to find the Dungeon exit. Working together, they managed to cover the remaining ground without issue, popping out just as the first bell of the afternoon had begun ringing. Their pronouncements generated quite a bit of controversy, especially when the bodies of their attackers were displayed to the guards.

Their losses—the Beastkin party losses—had been heavy. Kord had died, his spine and blood vessels severed. He had bled out while Daniel had been unable to see and heal him. Pol was lost too, knocked off the edge of the island. Thankfully, Oak had been saved as had Wasme, who had collapsed soon after the battle was over.

The entire fight had taken only a few minutes, but so many had fallen. The team that had attacked them had likely expected to have an unfair, overwhelming advantage from their enchantments and had failed to take into account how many of the Beastkin could see in the dark. That they had found the enchanted necklace of darkness—now held in the hands of Wasme—had been of little advantage. Nor would the provision of the attacking team's equipment. Goods were not sufficient trade for lives, not unless you were entirely too mercantile and cold.

Certainly not for Daniel. He mentally cursed himself, wishing he had done more. None of the opposing team had even attempted to harm him or Omrak. And hearing what they had said, he wondered if they would have been attacked if they had joined. If they had been braver, if they had tried to get involved, would Kord still live? Would Pol?

What ifs. One of the greatest opponents for an Adventurer, especially after a staggering loss like this one. All too easy to fall into the spiral of recrimination, to ask yourself what you could have done better. And hindsight always offered better options, better methods. Better choices.

Long periods of interrogation and questioning were the result of their reports, conducted both separately and together. In the end, however, the Guild released them all. The bodies had provided no clue about the team's employers and with a single, ambiguous sentence, the entirety of the clues provided, the Guild and the City Guard could do nothing but send them on their way. Not that deep investigation was something either conducted normally.

In truth, investigating wrongs was a difficult and expensive proposition. Most times, the guard's job was dealing with the aftereffects of theft, robbery, and the like. The occasional thief or pickpocket caught in the act was the extent of their policing activity. The few Investigators that they had were often busy with bigger, more important crimes than dealing with an Adventurer-only matter.

As for the Guild—what happened in a Dungeon stayed in the Dungeon. While they discouraged and would ban any Adventurer caught preying on one another, such vendettas were a fact of life. There was little they could do, since a full Dungeon could be multiple times the size of even a city as large as Silverstone. Theirs was a risky occupation and with it, certain dangers were considered common.

It was knowing all this why Daniel found it frustrating that his questioning had taken so long. As the main focus of the investigation, he had been dragged aside to be interviewed vigorously for hours on end. Answering the same questions multiple times in different ways, always cognizant that he had a secret that he did not desire to reveal was draining. But finally, finally, he was free.

Only to be met, as he walked out from the passageway leading from the interview rooms, by the giant Bearkin. Wasme looked tired, his cheeks sunken, his eyes red.

"Are you okay?" Daniel asked. He reached out to touch the other, concern making him want to check on the Bearkin, only to watch Wasme flinch from his hand. "Wasme?"

"I must rescind the offer, Daniel," Wasme said.

"Offer?" Daniel said. "To the Broken Chain?"

"Yes. I received . . . other word, while we were waiting. Between our losses and . . . other matters . . . we cannot offer you what you need." Wasme ducked his head, looking embarrassed for a second. "I'm sorry."

Daniel blinked, feeling a little hurt and whiplashed by the sudden change in Wasme's demeanour. "Can you, can you tell me what's going on?"

"I'm sorry, no. It's guild business." Wasme shook his head. "Just know it's not personal. And be careful."

Wasme turned away, stomping off. Daniel watched his fading back, brows furrowed in thought. Eventually, he made his way out to the tavern to find Asin and Omrak sitting at a table with an untouched mug of ale awaiting him. As he took a seat with his friends, he noticed them glaring at a corner. Turning his head, he found Mattias sipping on his drink and looking back at the pair. When Mattias was certain he had caught Daniel's eyes, he raised the drink in salute.

Anger flared, and Daniel half-stood, only stopped by a hand on his arm by Asin. She shook her head and pushed down his appendage, urging the healer to sit. Eventually, he sank back down in his seat before he leaned forward to speak to his friends.

"It was him, wasn't it?" Daniel said.

"Yes." Asin said.

"We should . . ." Daniel trailed off as his good sense caught up with him. He knew there was nothing they could do. After all, they had no evidence. A friendly nod in the tavern was not considered evidence. Certainly not to accuse another Adventurer in good standing or the guild he represented.

"If we were in the North, I would challenge him to a duel," Omrak rumbled. "Draw my sword and—"

"Be cut down." A familiar voice spoke up from behind the big Northerner. A second later, Nicole Novak, guildmaster of the smaller Bent Nail, had plopped herself down with the team, followed soon after by a pair of her guildmates. "You're no match for him."

"I . . ."

"Trust me. He's a Violet-level Advanced Classer who specialises in duels," Nicole said. She turned around, offering Mattias a smile. Mattias bent his head in return to the guildmistress before returning to his drink. Nicole blithely continued on as she spoke. "He's who the Three Skills send when they are having troubling negotiating an equitable deal."

Asin let out a chuff at that, half amused, half angry.

"Should you be sitting with us?" Daniel said, worriedly. He'd picked up the strange tension in the room, though he'd initially dismissed it as the usual concerns whenever word of a hunting party arose. Now, he was not so sure.

"Nice of the young ones to care," Nicole said, smiling at Daniel. "But it's fine. He's already made his threats, and we've already confirmed we're not looking for a healer. Not one that the Three Skills is so desperate to acquire."

"You too?" Daniel said, dismayed.

"Us too." Nicole inclined her head. "We're a small guild, overall. And while we could stand most kinds of pressure . . . or displeasure, the kind he's bringing to bear . . ." Nicole's eyes grew dark, the lightness she was using to answer the questions disappearing for a second, shadows in her eyes. "Well, let's just say that I left the capital for a reason."

"You were in the capital?" Daniel said, surprised.

"Yes."

The curt answer from Nicole killed the conversation, leaving the table awkwardly silent. After a second, Asin leaned forward and fixed Daniel in the eye. When he looked over, she spoke slowly, carefully enunciating each word. "Sorry. Chain wrong. I . . . wrong. Thought help."

"Help who?" Daniel said, frustration bubbling within him. At being threatened, his life put in danger, people killed. Over his idiotic, stupid Gift. And, perhaps, a little at himself for being so careless with its content. "Me or the Chain?" Asin flinched a little, her ears folding down and her tail wrapping close around her body. "You could have made that offer at any time, but you decided to keep it quiet until now. And look where that got us!"

Asin stopped flinching at the last, going unnaturally still. Then, she bared her teeth—all too sharp—at Daniel and hissed at him. The next moment, she had sprung from her chair and headed out the door.

"That was uncalled for," Nicole said from where she sat.

"And who's asking you?" Daniel growled, shoving his untouched mug of ale away. It sloshed out, spilling all over the table as he stood up. "Not as if you're much of a help either."

Before Omrak could say anything, he strode out.

As he exited, he could not help but notice Mattias in the corner, grinning. Making his smouldering anger rage even further, until he exited the Guild Hall and he started running. To where, he was not entirely certain. But anywhere was better than the Ba'al-cursed hall and the useless Adventurers within.

***

Days passed with Daniel staying away from the hall. He spent his time training at one of the local training yards, working with a trainer on his technique with mace and shield and the rest of his time in the hospice. He read his books when he had a few moments, studying additional diseases and cures while he worked the never-ending press of humanity. He worked fervently, trying to dismiss intrusive thoughts and the piles of declined invitations to meet from other guilds.

Those kept coming, invitations rescinded even when he asked them. Once they were desperate for him to join, now he could not even get a meeting with their guildmaster. Even the Green Robin had declined his invitation, leaving just three guilds: the Red Robin, who were waiting for their Guildmaster; the Three Skills; and the Seven Stones.

Not many options, especially after what had happened. Daniel continued to receive rumors from the few Adventurers who came by, seeking free healing. One of the rumors that abounded was how the Guild had not found further information on the hunting party. Another was how other guilds were being warned off.

And the growing rumor that Daniel's skill in healing was not just simple spells.

Perhaps, if he had more time, if he had gained greater strength, his options would have widened. If he was more than a mediocre melee fighter and a vague healer. But, instead, he was left with these few, for few would dare step between him and the royalty. And even fewer had strength to actually make the royals accept their demands.

Eventually though, a letter arrived that Daniel could not ignore. That morning, the sealed envelope with the red stamp of a pair of roses lay waiting for him when he arrived for breakfast. And rather than leave, to avoid his friends, he stayed seated at his breakfast table.

Asin was the first down, plopping in a seat next to him without a word. She sat there in silence until the tavern keeper had deposited her meal—sliced steak strips from leftovers last night with a heavy spice seasoning addition and puffy, freshly baked bread—before uttering her first word.

"Thanks."

The tavern keeper blinked, surprised since the silent Catkin normally just offered a nod. He muttered his own agreement before disappearing into the kitchen again, his morning clientele demanding his time. Asin dug into her meal, still blatantly ignoring Daniel.

Shifting in his seat uncomfortably, he looked around, taking in the mixture of travelling merchants and Adventurers that made up the clientele of this tavern. Most of the merchants ignored him, the occasional bodyguard glancing around as they supped next to their employers. The Adventurers, on the other hand, were more curious, though most knew better than to bother the pair. Healing—if Daniel had any Mana to spare—was in the evening, not the mornings.

No matter how bad the hangovers were.

As Omrak, clambering down the stairs and nursing his head, well knew. He stopped on the final step, having realized that Daniel was still present. The Northerner did not hesitate beyond his initial surprise, stomping over and sitting down.

"So. Are you done being angry with us? Or should I find a new party?" Omrak rumbled, crossing his arms.

Asin looked up, her ears swiveling forwards as her tail slowed in its swinging. Jade eyes fixed upon Daniel, waiting for his answer.

"I might have been in the wrong . . ." Daniel said, scratching his head embarrassedly. "I was just so angry . . ."

"Anger is fine. Just do not take it out on us," Omrak said. "We too are enraged by the actions of those without honor."

Asin nodded.

"Yeah. I'm sorry. And you were right, Asin. I would never have agreed to join the Broken Chain earlier either," Daniel said, ashamedly. "Not because of anything . . . I just, I'm worried. About you-know-what."

Another nod from the Catkin.

"It is a heavy burden to bear, Friend Daniel," Omrak rumbled.

Daniel offered a wry smile in answer, then pushed the still-sealed envelope forwards. "Anyway. We received a reply. I thought you'd want to be here when we read it."

"Then let us read it!" Omrak said. Daniel reached for the envelope, breaking the seal and scanning the words over. He frowned, before handing it over to Asin even as the large Northerner almost seemed to vibrate in impatience. "Well?"

"It's from the Red Roses . . ." Daniel broke off, waiting for Omrak's food to be delivered before he continued. "It's about our application."

"Yes. Stop standing on the cliff's edge! It's time to jump," Omrak said, ignoring the food before him as he leaned forward.

"They want us to meet their people and do another delve," Daniel said, his voice lowering unconsciously.

"Good!" roared Omrak, pounding the table. Their drinks sloshed and a painful creak resounded as the table struggled to stay together. The proprietor glared at Omrak, who offered an abashed grin. "Fear is for the cowardly. Honor is more important."

Daniel grimaced at his friend's boisterous exclamation. He wondered exactly how well-prepared the Red Roses were, but decided he was not going to poke at the good fortune too much. After all, they had gone as far as to ask from their main Guild. Whatever choice they had made, it was obvious that they had the full backing of their guild, which was something even the Seven Stones had not been able to agree to.

"When?" Asin, ever practical, asked.

"This afternoon," Daniel said. He frowned a little, at both the speed and lack of warning for this event and that they were entering in the middle of the day. Not that the day-night schedule of the Dungeon lined up with the world outside, but most Adventurers preferred to try to keep their own schedules aligned with the external world. Going in now would mean a short trip or an extended one. Or maybe they just didn't care.

"Ready." Asin placed a hand on her chest, indicating who she meant. Then she focused on finishing the food set before her.

"Aye. I have nothing that cannot be put aside for another day."

"Then we meet this afternoon," Daniel said. He paused, then flashed the group a sheepish grin. "And, thank you. Again."

Grunts and slurps were all that greeted his apology, making the healer smile. Friends, good friends, might fight, but they also accepted apologies when you were done. And guarded your back when you needed it.

***

Fire. The team excelled at using fire. Daniel watched as they literally strolled through the second level of Porthos, blowing apart flocks of Imps in expanding fireballs of flame, erupting from enchanted arrows and bolts. Three different archers worked the surroundings while a pair of swordsmen guarded the sides of the team and those in the center where the support personnel and Daniel's team were deployed.

Perhaps most interesting to Daniel was the single Mage who walked alongside them all, an enchanted wire contraption with a globe in the middle and a pouch in the center. All around them Imps died and dissipated into smoke while Mana stones zipped through the air, drawn to the globe before falling into the pouch.

"Wonderful item," Daniel said, gesturing at the enchanted contraption. "Though I'm surprised you're able to power it for so long."

"It only needs a little Mana. Most of it is drawn from the surroundings of the Dungeon," Eleanor said, running a hand through her short red hair. "A single dedicated Mage can keep it powered easily from their natural regeneration, as long as they focus. More expensive Gatherers can be powered with an actual Mana stone, but for our purposes, this works."

Daniel watched as another stone flew through the air, swerving around Omrak before sliding into the center and being deposited. "I can see how it'd be useful in this dungeon. But it seems very situational. And expensive."

"It is." Eleanor nodded. "An advantage of being in a Guild, and one with connections. We are able to acquire such items and invest in the future of the guild. And you'd be surprised at the use such a piece of equipment has. Underwater dungeons, ones fought in rivers and even dark-aspected dungeons all make such tools useful. For those high-level teams who seek to acquire funds, there are even enchanter guilds that rent out such equipment on a weekly basis."

"High-level teams?" Omrak rumbled. "Should they not have sufficient funds already running Master-level dungeons?"

"Not really. Master-level dungeons are expensive and dangerous. A single mistake, a lack of preparation, could end their lives easily," Eleanor replied. "Most Master-Class teams actually run Advanced Dungeons to build up funds. Rushing through a full Dungeon and clearing it repeatedly is safer and more profitable overall."

"Fascinating," Omrak said. He frowned, jerking his head back even as another Mana stone swerved around him. "How are they avoiding me?"

"Good enchanting. And your aura. You can think of it as strings pulling the stones to the Gatherer, strings that bend around your aura."

"Fascinating." Omrak repeated himself.

Daniel shook his head, turning over the tactics he was seeing. As the echo of another explosion died off, the wash of heat warming his face one last time, he continued. "We're making great time here, but are you even earning enough?" He gestured at a nocked bow and the enchanted arrow. "Those must be expensive."

"Less than you'd think," Eleanor said. "But again, it's a matter of Guild ability. We have our own Enchanters. They make such arrows for us, at the cost of time and a minor profit. In turn, we are able to clear floors faster, allowing our members to gain a larger amount of experience in a shorter period. With the Gatherer, we generally make a small profit."

"How small?" Asin asked, as she prowled alongside the team.

"Mmm . . . a couple of gold for a single-day run," Eleanor said. "On average."

"Person?"

"No, for the team."

Daniel winced. That was horrendous. It was the kind of profit he would expect for a Beginner Adventurer, not an Advanced-Class team.

"Don't forget, you get free room and board," Eleanor said. "And our teams Level and clear Dungeons faster and safer."

A roar from up ahead made her smile, as she gestured to where they spotted the Floor Boss. Within seconds, both archers had targeted and fired upon the distant monster, triggering skills to **Replicate** even the enchanted arrows. The explosions that erupted knocked the monster around, making it emerge from the attack badly scorched and missing an arm. A single normal arrow using a **Penetrating Shot** that buried itself in the monster's forehead ended the battle before it could even truly begin. A few seconds of manipulation later, and the Mana Stones flew towards them, even as muffled curses came from the rest of the team at not finding the floor chest.

That probably was somewhere else or already stolen.

"See? Easy."

"I do . . ." Daniel said, his voice edged with doubt still. He did see, but he could not help but glance at the bored-looking swordsmen that flanked the team. They chatted with one another, ignoring Daniel's team, paying more attention and flirting with each other than watching for trouble.

Yet, as the lead member of the team waved them towards the dungeon stairs headed down, Daniel could not help but admit they were right. This really was effective.

***

Hours later, they emerged from the Dungeon. Other than a single—brief—moment of danger on the fourth floor where they had been ambushed, leading to a flurry of attacks and the use of health potions by the injured members of the Red Roses, the entire trip had passed with little fanfare or excitement.

Eleanor led them to a quiet meeting room, blowing past Mattias who glared at the group, his lips peeled back in a silent snarl. Once they were within and seated, she faced the team.

"You've seen what our training is like. This is what we will want from you." Eleanor held up a graceful hand. "Firstly, you will join our teams and work with them on leveling in the city. Your current Level is too low for our needs, especially your Mana." Daniel opened his mouth to ask how she knew, and she continued to speak right over him. "Yes, we perused your Status Screen. We have people who can do that. Now be quiet until I finish."

Asin hissed and Daniel glared, but he did keep silent. Omrak just looked uncomfortable.

"You will all need to learn some etiquette. Such remedial classes will be provided for all of you. Attendance and passing will be mandatory," Eleanor continued. "You may continue training at the hospice, though you will reduce the time you spend there to only—at most—three days a week. The rest of the time will be spent healing and studying in the Guild. A tutor will be provided. Once you have dedicated at least two more Levels to your healing spells and gained a minimum of three new spells including **Heal Moderate Wounds**, the restrictions will lift, and you may choose your other proficiencies." Daniel's face grew bleaker at each word, his hand curling into a fist as they sat upon the table. Eleanor flicked a glance at the fist but she continued. "This is the start of your build. We will likely have other requirements as you grow, but such discussions will be held after you achieve your next few Levels.

"As for your team, you may continue to stay together. Your friends can act as our melee safeguards, while we will also provide two additional support personnel—a Mage and one other—and three ranged attackers." Pausing briefly, Eleanor consulted notes within her mind. "That will mean your Catkin—Asin—will be required to alter her build and strengthen her melee forms. A longer series of weapons will be required."

"Scout?" Asin hissed.

"Not required. You will no longer be exploring new Dungeons. Each of your delves will be in Dungeons whose layouts we have ascertained." She ticked her fingers off. "You'll also stop taking exploration or other quests without approval from the Guild. For the most part, I expect they will be refused unless they are healing Quests." A slight inclination of her head. "Plague quests in particular will likely be the kinds we expect the royals and other nobles will require of you."

Daniel winced but nodded. It was not as if he would turn down a plague quest if one came up. Thankfully, those were relatively rare and handled by the Clerics and Healers. But if one grew to require the Adventurers Guild, it would be bad.

"Is that it?" Daniel asked.

"In the majority," Eleanor said, nodding. "You will also be required to provide occasional healing at the request of the guildmaster or guild heads, but those will be dependent upon the extent of your Gift. For example—can you heal missing parts?" Daniel shook his head, and Eleanor's lips pursed. "Well, pity. But not unexpected. We shall be testing the limits to better understand what and where you'll be needed."

"And the Three Skills?" Daniel asked, forcing the words out. He was still angry at the high-handed way she—the guild—was arranging his life, but maybe it was the start of the negotiations. And in negotiating, everything could change. So of course they asked for more.

"We will deal with them. They might have some modicum of influence with the royals, but we have the backing of many more nobles," Eleanor said. "If we accept you in, we will be able to handle them."

Daniel nodded and she extracted a document, dropping it on the table. "The full details are here. Understand, the details might be negotiable, but the intent is not. If you join us, you will do what we ask you to do."

"Are we just your dogs, then?" Omrak said.

"Tools. Useful tools, but tools nonetheless," Eleanor said, sniffing. "And that is Daniel. You two" —she looked at Omrak and Asin— "are not even that. Yet. If you gain strength, then you may have the right to consider yourself more. Till then, I would not be so rude. After all, you came to us."

Daniel gestured at his friend, getting him to shut up while Eleanor walked out. When she did leave, Omrak burst out in angry cursing while Daniel forced himself to breathe and peruse the document. He was rather upset at the way they had been treated. Whether Eleanor was doing so because she was angry at them or just did not want them to join, he was uncertain. But at least the document was not significantly different from what had been discussed. Just more detailed.

As Omrak finally wound down, Asin cleared her throat. "So?"

"What did you think of their teamwork?" Daniel said, avoiding answering the question directly.

"Effective," Asin said. "Boring."

"Very much so," Omrak rumbled, dissatisfied. "There is no honor nor glory in their delving. They might as well be selling potatoes or making cheese." At Daniel's raised eyebrow, the Northerner waved his hand. "Honorable professions and actions. But *boring*."

Daniel smiled. "Yes. That's the word, isn't it. I do not think we'd learn much, joining them. They might be safe and effective, but there is no thrill in their work."

"Three Skills."

The purr-growl from Asin made Daniel's face fall before he nodded. "Yes. But at least they can handle the Three Skills. And I'd rather join boring than evil."

"Then we should speak with them, Friend Daniel."

"Who?" Daniel frowned.

"The Seven Stones," Omrak said. "For they are the only other choice."

Daniel sighed, but nodded. Truth. They were the only other option, and if that was the case, they might as well get it over with. Ask and verify. And if they would take them, then they would.

"Then, let's go." He stood up, walking to the exit from the room. No more choices, no more hesitation. Time to just make a decision and get it done.

He was just worried, a little, how Mattias would react.

Chapter 11

The trio were within a few blocks of the Seven Stones guild residence when they were waylaid by Mattias. Unlike the other times they had met the man, he was accompanied this time by a quartet of other individuals, all of them rough-looking with dirty, disheveled faces, unkempt hair, and worn armor. There were even a number of prominent bloodstains on each of their clothes and armor, to Daniel's disgust.

"And where do you think you're going?" Mattias's voice was cold now, no longer as urbane or congenial as it had been upon their first meeting.

Daniel frowned, coming to a stop as his attempt to step around the group was blocked by the thugs who spread out further. He frowned, curious how strong they were, frustrated there was no easy way to tell. In either case, they were outnumbered and Mattias was dangerous, or so they were told. It would likely take all of them just to beat him.

"On a walk," Daniel said.

"In the guild district?" Mattias said, his eyes raking contemptuously over the various guild residences around them. The entire district was made up of larger lots with gates blocking off views to the residences and training grounds hidden behind. "Looking for more help? Or something else . . ."

Daniel just smiled tightly.

"Yes, you're still trying to find a way around it. And after I've been so patient and generous," Mattias said, stepping closer. Daniel took a half step back before he forced himself to stop. His aborted movement made the other man smile mockingly at him.

"Why are you so insistent I join you anyway?" Daniel shook his head. "You didn't care as much before."

"Well, let's just say some new information has made itself known. Now I've been ordered to make sure you join us."

"Whether I want to or not?"

"Oh, no. We don't coerce guildmembers." Mattias shook his head, putting on a mock mournful expression that was as authentic as a peddler's cure-all. "That would be wrong. No, we much prefer it if our guild members understand they should join us."

Daniel's eyes flicked to the side as the thugs laughed uproariously at Mattias's words. Omrak stepped away to clear some space, growling and flexing his muscles. One of the thugs, nearly as large as Omrak, turned and faced the young Northerner, sneering as a sap appeared in his hand. Asin hissed, her tail lashing behind her.

"And is this how you intend to convince us? These men and the ones in the Dungeon?" Daniel's voice grew heated.

"What ones in the Dungeon?" Mattias said, innocently.

Daniel shook his head, his head turning to take in the pedestrians walking around. Many hurried away, obviously sensing the upcoming danger. But there were a few Adventurers, including a few who had exited their residences to stand outside their gates watching the entire proceedings. He doubted they'd help, but they might. It was one thing to threaten and launch attacks in the Dungeon, another to do so in the middle of the city.

"Well, if that's all you had to say, we'd like to keep walking," Daniel said. He winced a little, realizing how he sounded. He should have just demanded they be let go instead of asking.

Mattias looked around, spotting the same people Daniel had. His lips curled up further, before his gaze fixed on Asin, his voice continuing. "You know, I do think that our offer has changed. We'll not want any mongrels in our guild."

Daniel growled, while Asin turned her jade eyes on Mattias.

He continued to smirk while speaking. "Not that it matters, after all. I think these mongrels are going to find themselves in trouble. Troubled by others," the Three Skills recruiter said, turning his head slightly to say the last sentences to the thugs behind.

"Oh yeah. I hear their guild is made up of old dry wood. As is their entire district. Old, dry wood. Quite easy to burn . . ." one of the thugs, a fellow with a long scar that ran down one side of his face, said. "I hear they had to build part of it back up just a few years ago after an unfortunate accident."

"Are you people serious?" Daniel said, exasperated. "In public. Like this?"

"I'm always very serious about public safety," the scarred thug said, smiling at Asin who hissed at him. "Especially for the lesser kind who might not understand their place."

"You know what, I'd rather die than join you," Daniel said, the anger that had been boiling over exploding forth. "You can forget about me joining you for any reason."

"Are you sure that is your answer?" Mattias said, his voice growing colder. "Because those are very definite words."

"Yes, I'm sure." Daniel leaned forward, his face almost touching the other. "On Erlis's blood and Kwan Yin's merciful hand, I'm serious."

"Well, that's that, then." Mattias stepped back, that cold grin breaking into something a little more natural. If no less vicious. "Let's go, boys."

Daniel stood staring, his jaw unhinged as he watched Mattias and his thugs leave. He turned to his friends, speaking up. "What the hell is going on?"

His friends could only shrug, even as Mattias and his group turned the corner and disappeared, leaving the trio to stare dumbly after them.

"Did they want me to not join them? Or did he just want me to say it out loud? Did he push me to do it on purpose?" Daniel muttered to his friends, only starting to walk when Asin prodded him with one clawed finger. The Catkin just shrugged at every single question while Omrak rumbled in puzzlement, his head turning from side to side.

"I smell politics," the blond Northerner grumbled and added, "And I would not trust that one to give up so easily."

"Yeah . . ." Daniel said. Though what could he do? Kill him?

Shivering at the thought, considering what they had done, he could not help but think it might really be his goal. Not to have him join but for him to be killed. After all, if there was one thing more dangerous than an unaffiliated healer, it was one that messed with the "natural" order of things.

Considering the potential enemies he had made, Daniel kept walking. In the end, he had made his decision, even if it seemed to have been prompted by the other. And what would come, would come.

***

The group arrived at the guild house for the Seven Stones soon after and were ushered in by one of the guards. To Daniel's surprise, rather than entering Gadi's own office, they were directed to the one next to it to find Gadi and another individual waiting for them. This office was much larger but felt smaller because it was cluttered with discarded weapons and armor pieces, piled haphazardly. The array of weapons was astounding, ranging from a wide variety of polearms to blunt weapons and swords of every kind and size. Armor, on the other hand, seemed to focus on plate armor, with the occasional underarmor and chainmail piece added. The one thing Daniel did not spot were papers or filing cabinets, unlike Gadi's own room.

By his side, Asin's nose was wrinkled, and she was rubbing it vigorously. Daniel could understand her reaction since the accumulated stench of unwashed pieces and sword oil had his own breathing hitched. He eyed the closed window directly behind the guildmaster, wishing it would open to at least air the place out. But neither Gadi nor the bear-like guildmaster seemed to notice the stench as they bickered.

" . . . you can't take another vacation! You just left."

"But that's why you're here!" the guildmaster complained.

"That doesn't matter. I can't sign all the documents that I gave you. You need to certify them before I submit them to the head office," Gadi said.

"Bah! You have my seal to do that for me," the guildmaster said, offering Gadi a wide-eyed stare. It was disconcerting for Daniel to see, considering how muscular and strong the man was.

"And I told you I won't do that. It's fraud!" Gadi said, exasperated.

"Guildmasters . . ." The guard tried again, speaking up. This time, the pair turned to the waiting group. "Adventurer Chai and his friends are here."

"Who?" the guildmaster said.

"The Healer. I told you about him already," Gadi said, rolling his eyes. He waved the guard out while pointing a finger at the guildmaster. "I informed you yesterday when you came back and even gave you the documentation. Don't you ever read anything I give you, Parndo?"

"Why would I? You just tell me if it's important," Parndo said with a roll of his eye. The muscular man turned, staring at the trio as he idly scratched at a raised scar on one shoulder. It was a jagged and puckered thing, disappearing around the corner of his broad shoulders and ducking under his ragged shirt. "So, a healer? Good. We can always use more."

Daniel stepped forward, bowing slightly. "Guildmaster Parndo. Vice-Guildmaster Gadi. I—we—wanted to check if our application has been accepted. With the agreed-upon matters?"

"Well . . ." Gadi paused, looking over at Parndo.

"What are you looking at me like that for?" Parndo rumbled. "He's a healer. The other one looks strong, and I'm no animalist. Beastkin are fine. Looks good to me."

"There's a complication."

Parndo rolled his eyes and extracted his fingers from the scratching. "Of course there is. He a killer or something?"

"No!" Daniel exclaimed.

"Then?" Parndo said.

"The Three Skills want him," Gadi said and hurried on when Parndo acted as if he was going to interrupt. "Daniel here has a Gift for healing. A very powerful one."

"Enough that they're throwing their weight around?" Parndo said, propping his chin up on his hand now. The table creaked alarmingly as he put his weight on it.

"Yes." Gadi leaned over. "I don't care, we can deal with them. Though we might find getting some materials harder. But they also started playing dirty."

"What kind of dirty?" Parndo rumbled, angry.

"Hunting teams."

"Again?" The guildmaster slapped a hand on the table, making it creak alarmingly and the weapons on it jump. A throwing knife, on the edge, fell over and rattled on the stone floor. "Those Goblin-lovers. They go too far. When will the Guild do something about them?"

"You know there's no proof," Gadi said.

"Bah!" Parndo turned and spat to the side, crossing his arms. "How bad do you think it'll be?"

Daniel watched the pair argue, a lump in his throat as he waited. Omrak, on the other hand, seemed more interested in the array of weapons, staring at each piece while being careful not to touch.

"Bad. Daniel's gifts are . . . unique."

Parndo turned and fixed the healer with a firm gaze. To his surprise, Daniel realized that the brunet guildmaster actually had striking sterling grey eyes. "How unique."

When Gadi moved to answer, he raised a hand, making the vice-guildmaster silence himself.

Caught out, Daniel gulped around a suddenly dry throat. He could feel the pressure the guildmaster exerted by his presence, now that it was turned on him. A skill perhaps? Or just age and experience? He was uncertain, but he felt it would be a bad idea to lie.

"Very. I don't need Mana to heal. Just . . . memory." Daniel paused, then continued. "I can heal many ailments that even healing magic is unable to target. At least, on the lower levels."

"Your Gift skips tiers."

"Yes."

"Very unique then." Parndo crossed his arms. "Spell equivalent?"

"At least a **Major Regeneration**," Daniel said, recalling how he fixed the Champion.

"Poisons?"

"Yes."

"Diseases?"

"Most."

"Curses?"

"No."

"Very unique." Parndo nodded. "They'll really want you."

"I know. They've told me as much," Daniel said.

"Threatened." Asin spoke up, breaking her silence. Parndo looked at her, and she added, "Just now."

"Interesting." Parndo shrugged. "Fine. You want to join us?" Daniel hesitated, and Parndo snorted. "What?"

"I . . ." Daniel shook his head, realizing that explaining his hesitations to be a bad idea. "Nothing."

Parndo, however, turned to stare at Gadi. The vice-guildmaster winced, touching his mustache for a second before he answered. "The other guilds in town have backed down after the

Three Skills threatened them. I do not think Adventurer Chai has a choice any longer."

"Hah!" Parndo said.

Daniel twitched, wondering if that would matter to the guildmaster. Some might find being the second choice—or only choice by default—to be insulting to their guild. At the least, it could affect their deal.

"Better for us. So, you joining us, yes?"

Daniel jerked a nod, resolving himself. Omrak, startled by a pointy claw in his side, jerked up and then hastily added to Asin's voiced agreement.

"Good. Then we're done." He waved them out. "Gadi, go help them."

The vice-guildmaster made a face but picked his way around the pile of weapons and armor to lead the trio out the door. Just before they left though, Parndo spoke up one last time.

"Book me an appointment with the Three Skills, will you?"

Gadi's lips pressed tight before he bowed and closed the door on the guildmaster, leaving Daniel with one last glimpse of the man already putting his head down on his desk to nap.

Chapter 12

Unable to keep quiet any longer, Daniel turned to Gadi and pointed behind him at the office they had just left. "Is he always like that?"

"Who? The guildmaster?" Gadi assumed a put-upon expression before nodding. "He is. He barely does any work, either . . ." He rubbed a hand through his hair before he shrugged. "But guild law says that every guild branch must be run by a Master Adventurer, so here we are."

"He's a Master Adventurer?" Omrak exclaimed.

"Aye. Weapon Master Class too." Gadi tilted his head, considering. "*If* you catch him in a good mood, you should get him to run a lesson for you. He might not be much of a bureaucrat, but he's a very good Adventurer."

He paused, hand on the door that he'd led them to, considering something.

He shook his head after a moment, pushing the door open instead and waving them through. "Go ahead. The secretaries will finish your applications and have it couriered to the Guild to make sure it's all official."

"So . . . that's it?" Daniel said, surprised. Somehow, he had expected more.

"What? You want fanfare and petals?" Gadi snorted. "We'll announce your joining later. After the guildmaster has had his chat with the Three Skills."

"Right, yes, of course." Daniel backtracked. By his side, Asin rolled her eyes and stalked past him, flopping herself down on a seat while Omrak gently guided his friend within.

"Thank you, Adventurer Gadi."

"It's Vice-Guildmaster Gadi now." Gadi smiled as he corrected Omrak, who took the rebuke with a good-natured smile. A moment later, the doors were shut, leaving the trio to stare at one another.

Omrak, rather than sitting down, walked over to the waiting refreshment table, exclaiming at the use of lemons within the glass of water and the watered-down ale that were waiting for them.

Rather than bringing individual glasses over, he brought the entire tray before serving the group.

"So . . . we're good with this, right?" Daniel said, suddenly nervous once more. He knew they had agreed but now that it was done . . .

Asin let out a snort, dipping her head to sip at the cup in her hand. On the other hand, her tail had stopped moving for a short moment before it continued its languid swish behind her.

Omrak, as always, was much more direct. "We agreed. This was our best option. As for the Three Skills, in our village we used to be raided by another, one further north. They came by every winter, after the harvest was in, when they had grown bored of staying at home. They'd clamber over the mountains, cross the pass and then strike us before we knew they were there. Three winters, again and again.

"Then my father came back. And when he heard what they had done, he gathered all the men, during the summer, clambered over the pass, arrived at their village, and then slayed all the men who raided us. They never bothered us again after that."

Daniel blinked, staring at his jovial and rather bloodthirsty friend in shock. When he eventually got his voice to work, he asked, "And what was the point of that story?"

"Sometimes, you have to bear what you have to before you grow strong enough to burn down their houses and make their minds up for them to not bother you ever again," Omrak said.

Again, Daniel nodded. He offered his friend a tentative half-smile, only to be interrupted by the entrance of a young, curvy female elf. She carried the series of papers with her and a small inscribing stone. That stone, Daniel knew, would be used on their Adventurer's passes to mark the fact that they had agreed to this. And, glancing at his friends, Daniel knew now that they had to. No more time for hesitating, no more vacillating.

They were going to join a guild.

Finally.

***

It didn't take them very long after that to fill out the paperwork. Once they were done and the young, shapely elf—though Daniel did wonder if she really was young, what with the ageless thing that they did—had left, Gadi returned, accompanied by the members of the team they had met, each of them looking both excited and a little worried.

First in was, of course, Lady Nyssa. The noblewoman was stopped short of sweeping in by her deaf bodyguard, the archer, who gripped a pair of crossed short swords before he let her in. Then, of course, came the healer, almost bouncing in. The young teenager grinned at Daniel as she entered, rushing over as she spoke. "You were so right! I'm leveling up my healing skill so fast, I'm going to break through to Beginner in months!"

Daniel smiled, watching as Zef and Harlow slid in, his eyes almost missing the shorter thief as he slunk into the room. "Good. Which hospice are you visiting?"

"The one just off Merchant Street," Anne replied.

Daniel nodded. That made sense. Safer than the one he visited, with its poor and the laborers. Those near Merchant Street worked with those with a little more money to their name. Or who were willing to act like they had, dressing up enough so that they weren't thrown out. "Good. Keep going as often as you can, especially when you have Mana to spare."

"Oh . . . I don't have a spell yet." Anne hung her head.

Daniel raised an eyebrow, and she hurriedly explained.

"I was told it was better to learn one manually. I've been taking classes when I can afford them," Anne replied.

Daniel sighed. That made sense. She probably was paying through her nose to learn, too, since most Healers hated to waste their time and add to the competition. The only reason they would be willing to help her was because she was an Adventurer and thus, less competition. Also, it was always useful to have an Adventurer that you knew. Sometimes, the enchanted equipment they found could be quite useful for non-Adventurers.

At the side, Lady Nyssa watched the pair chatter, her lips compressed into a tight angry line. Asin watched the entire group silently, Zef having taken a seat beside her. Daniel idly noted that unlike the Catkin's slowly swaying tail, the Lizardkin's tail was not moving. Tense? Or just not as energetic as mammals? If he considered what lizards were like, perhaps the second.

"Ahem." Gadi cleared his throat, drawing their attention. When Anne shut up, having started relating some of the cases she had seen, the vice-guildmaster nodded. "Now, you know each other. We can, of course, find others if they are unsuitable. But I wanted you to consider them first . . ."

The trio nodded, sharing long looks. Then, Asin pointed at Harlow and shook her head. The thief, who had been lounging behind the group at a wall, trying to stay hidden, blinked. "What? What'd you have against me?" Harlow said, frowning. "It's because I was a thief, right?"

Asin shook her head and pointed at herself. "Scout." She pointed at him. "Scout."

Then she just repeated her gesture of negation.

"Some teams have dual scouts. And Harlow does have some skills you lack. He's very adept at lock-picking," Gadi said, even as Harlow bristled.

"Learn."

It took everyone a few seconds to realize what she meant.

"Well, I guess we can arrange for teachers." Asin nodded at Gadi's words. "I'm sorry, Harlow. It seems we'll still have to find you a team."

"Whatever. Not as if I care." Saying that, the thief flounced out of the room, making Daniel crack a little smile. He spotted the older bodyguard doing the same.

"Mmm . . . Zef is good. Another frontline fighter would be useful," Omrak said, rubbing his chest. "As we journey deeper, the lower levels grow harder."

There were nods at that while Daniel tried to squash his own irritation. He was not a front-line fighter. Not really. They had discussed that. Still, he hated the idea.

"Thank you. It'll be good to be in a new party." Yellow eyes with its pupils slitted turned to fix on Asin for a brief moment before he continued. "And I believe we should have no trouble."

Gadi just grunted, rubbing at his nose while Daniel considered the implications. Perhaps he'd have to keep an eye on his friend. And find out from Zef how bad it was for Beastkin.

Beside him, Anne squirmed, eyes wide as she stared up at him. He snorted, but nodded at her, which resulted in a loud whoop from the young lady. She even went so far as to throw her hands up in the air, making Asin let out a loud chuff and Omrak laugh uproariously. Even Zef snickered, while Lady Nyssa flushed red in embarrassment for the young girl.

Eventually, her celebrations were over, leaving Gadi to pointedly stare at the trio and the only remaining member of the party that they had yet to discuss. Omrak was the first to begin.

"We have five now. That's a good number," the Northerner rumbled.

"No magic," Asin pointed out.

"But we'd have to add two." Omrak paused, looked at Nyssa, who gave him a quick nod of confirmation. "That's seven. Very large party."

"And the shrieking," Daniel said, tapping his ears. "That hurts."

Asin nodded quickly at that. With her own abilities, it was clear that she was more sensitive to the attacks.

Lady Nyssa tilted her head upwards, growing colder with each word. By her side, her bodyguard stirred, but she placed a hand on his arm, making him stop moving. Daniel noted how he turned his head constantly, to keep track of who was speaking, to read their lips. A good trick.

"I can provide my permanent team artifacts to help with my spells," Lady Nyssa spoke up, making Gadi look at her in surprise. "Not immediately, of course, for everyone. Even my father did not expect such a large party."

The team glanced at one another, but it was Daniel who spoke up. "Too many enchantments can conflict with one another, you know."

"These are particularly well made." She flicked her gaze to below his waist where his hammer hung and then Asin's bracers. "And I'm sure by the time we have an issue, you all will have progressed further. As would my control."

Daniel turned to his friends, eyes glinting with a little bit of amusement. The others stared at him before they all nodded.

"I miss Rob. His abilities were very versatile. And while she isn't, a Mage can be useful," Omrak said. "I say take her on. For now."

"Enough," Asin said, letting out a chuff and tapping a clawed finger on the table. Gadi winced, eyeing the spot and hoping she had not marred the finish. "No teasing. Take her."

"Well, I guess that's decided. You're both in," Daniel said, nodding to the pair. In truth, adding a second archer to the team would shore up one of their biggest weaknesses. Along with the magic, they would be able to handle the lower levels.

Or at least, that was the thought.

As he stared at the grinning group, Daniel found himself smiling back in turn. Perhaps this would work out, joining a guild. Forming a team.

Certainly, they had a couple of Dungeons they needed to finish. And now, perhaps, they could.

Chapter 13

Daniel ducked, snarling as the Swift Ape Alpha swung at him. Somehow, he had ended up facing the monster rather than Zef and Omrak, like they were meant to. Now he was doing his best to hold the massive creature off, its fetid breath washing over him with each shriek, the muskiness of its scent and untamed fur encompassing him like its blizzard of attacks.

Each second, Daniel ducked and wove and occasionally, when he had no choice, blocked the attack with his shield. His arms ached, his hammer barely doing more than supporting his own defense. Once in a while, he found an opening to strike out, but the monster's thick fur and its corded muscles blunted the majority of his attacks.

Perin's Blow had already been used and was recharging. **Double Strike** had been wasted, the monster nearly tearing the hammer out of his hands when he had used it. As for his **Find Weakness** ability, it flashed up spots constantly, but Daniel was just not fast enough to get in. Only **Shield Bash** was of any use, helping to keep the monster from overwhelming him.

An arrow drilled past his shoulder, nearly hitting him. By this point, the healer had gotten used to the buzzing arrows fired by the bodyguard and did not let his own concentration waver. He knew the rest of the team was dealing with the flood of Swift Apes the Alpha had called down on them, so he just had to hang on. In the meantime, he trusted the bodyguard and his skill **Guard's Foreknowledge** to estimate where he would be and ensure he was not hit.

To avoid another blow coming down overhand, Daniel hopped aside, catching the sight of Lady Nyssa standing arms akimbo. She was tossing orbs of **Empowered Noise** into the background so the attacks were happening on a level deeper and lower than his hearing could sense. It caused loose rocks to jump and his teeth to ache, but the monsters in proximity to the orbs were bleeding from their eyes and noses.

Omrak, on the other hand, was having the time of his life, his body glowing red. He had taunted a large portion of the monsters to him and was now swinging his double-handed sword around in sweeping cuts that cut at skin and disemboweled those that neared him. Already, his entire body pulsed with red rage attack, ready for him to unleash **The Lightning's Call.**

A shadow flashed by, stopping long enough to duck under an outstretched hairy arm. A blade cut, slashing at the hamstring of the monster and leaving a thin line of blood. Then the Catkin bounced away, long before the Alpha could retaliate at her properly. Knives were withdrawn and tossed at more Swift Apes, distracting and harrying the ones attempting to push past the blockade that Zef wove with his spear. Behind him, Anne had crawled up a rocky outcropping to fire down at the Apes, occasionally ducking as one of the Apes found a rock to toss at her.

Daniel had no time to pay attention to any of that. With the Alpha distracted, he threw himself forward and swung his hammer down with his full strength. He used the spiked side on the hammer, hoping to drive it into the monster's back.

And, to his surprise, succeeding.

Even knowing he had hit a critical portion of its body, his spike sliding between ribs and lodging deep, Daniel never expected to be as successful. And when the Alpha twirled around to strike him, Daniel kept hold of his hammer.

"Aaaarggghhhhhhhhhhhh!"   Daniel screamed as he was swung around, hanging on to the embedded hammer and a tight grip on its fur as the monster tried to grab him. Eyes wide, Daniel could only hope for his friends to come and save him.

***

"An unconventional fighting method," Lady Nyssa said, staring down at Daniel's sprawled form.

Beside him, the Swift Ape Alpha's body that had finally been slain was dissipating, drawn into the hammer by pure luck. That brought a smile to Daniel's face even as he attempted to regain his breath. He understood her sarcasm, but really, he didn't care.

Working on Omrak, Anne was scolding the big man. "Just hold still, I'll have you bandaged in a second." His area effect skill had taken out nearly a third of the Swift Apes by itself but had left the big Northerner more injured than usual.

Out of the corner of his eye, Daniel eyed his friend's health and watched as the poultices and bandages made the blond Northerner's health tick up a little. It would not rise much; there was only so much good food and medicine could do in the short term, and a **Healer's Mark** would take care of the rest . . . when he found his breath.

Padded feet passed by him, scooping up the Alpha's gemstone before it continued onwards to join the bodyguard. The silent bodyguard—

deaf, but rarely choosing to speak—had taken on Mana stone collecting duties with Asin, though the Catkin continued to hold the team's treasure.

"How long are we to rest?" Zef asked. The scaled warrior was mostly uninjured. He was seated against the wall, a strip of dried meat in hand as he snacked.

"Slave drivers," Daniel muttered under his breath. He pushed himself up, nodding in thanks to Lady Nyssa when she helped him, and watched as she walked off to meditate and regain some Mana. The young Mage had grown more adept at her spells as time went on, but managing Mana use through a Dungeon run was important. "Ten minutes. We need to let Omrak's **Healer's Mark** settle first."

"What **Healer's Mark?**" Anne said, bouncing on the tips of her toes.

"That one," Daniel said, finishing his cast. Omrak pulsed for a second before the spell caught and kept building within him.

The teenager pouted, upset by the fact that she missed him casting again. Not that she wouldn't get enough chances to watch him. After all, this was only their second run down a Dungeon. And thus far, they still needed a lot of practice to make sure their team gelled.

Even if they were pushing through floors faster.

Fourth floor next, Daniel thought with some contentment. They were finally progressing again.

***

Fourth floor of Aramis. Their first change of biome. More humanoid monsters, these were catlike—similar to the catlike Asin—but much less sentient. With stripes of black across yellow fur, they were larger than Asin by far, going for a much larger appearance, and significantly more bestial. They did not even stand to their full height but hunched over in all their movements.

often reverting to full sprints on all four limbs when they had the chance.

The Bajang were fearsome, their strength easily equaling the Swift Apes the level above. Worse than that, though, was the fact that the Bajang were stealth predators and more prone to attacking when individuals were unaware than straight up fights. Added to their incredible speed, this meant that most parties would see at least one or two successful sneak attacks, leaving the party members injured and potentially dead. The Bajang would retreat, carrying the still-struggling bodies with them, which led to a higher-than-normal death count for this level.

The fact that the fourth to sixth biome was a mixed jungle-and-cave biome added to the difficulty of the level. Large caverns and tight pathways with high sloping walls offered the prowling monsters multiple locations to hide and attack from before slinking away through small tunnels between passages difficult to spot and traverse.

"And you're sure this will work?" Daniel said, frowning as Lady Nyssa held the ball before her. The floating silver ball would pulse every few seconds before returning to quiescent.

"Yes. The Orb of Soh-Nah is a Silver-ranked artifact. I wouldn't even be allowed to use it if any of my family members had a propensity to **Sound Magic**," Lady Nyssa said. "But we have multiple accounts of its use in this dungeon from previous periods, as well as in general."

"Noisy," Asin complained, rubbing at her ear.

"I don't hear anything," Omrak said. Beside him, Zef nodded in agreement.

"It's pitched at a much higher range than *most* humanoid hearing," Lady Nyssa explained. She looked at Asin consideringly. "However, if you can hear it, maybe a little adjustment . . ."

Biting her lip, she pressed upon the orb for a few seconds. The next time it pulsed, Asin didn't wince, but nodded.

"And how will it work?" Daniel asked.

"It'll inform its user of potential threats. I get a . . . map . . . of the world imprinted in my mind. Anything that is attempting to move through it, I should sense. I need to only make a few adjustments to highlight the Bajang and I'll be able to spot them," Lady Nyssa said.

"Good," Daniel said, looking relieved. He had heard more than enough stories and had healed a number of wounds for unlucky Adventurers. The long claw wounds and the deep teeth marks were enough of a warning.

Shortly, the group shook itself out and began their slow and careful traversal through the floor. Unlike other labyrinth-like locations, the caverns and rooms on the second biome for the Dungeon did not alter themselves very much on a daily basis. Instead, the Dungeon moved the stairs down. As such, while every team that entered the second biome had a map of the floor, each day they still had to traverse the twisting, shrouded corridors in search of the staircase and the way down.

It did not take longer than fifteen minutes before Lady Nyssa indicated they were being stalked. It was another ten before the creature finally decided to try to end them. Unfortunately, with its cover blown and the Mage using hand signs to keep everyone updated, when the Bajang finally chose to leap off a nearby outcropping, bursting out from behind a conveniently located fern, Lady Nyssa's bodyguard was able to put an arrow into it and Zef to stab it. Pinned and crippled, the majestic bestial humanoid monster was quickly ended with minimal injuries.

Each battle after that was similar, with the team delving deeper and deeper.

Perhaps luck was with them too, since it took them only an hour and a half to find the way down, leaving them to plunge deeper onto the fifth floor where more Bajangs in greater numbers awaited. Considering how little impediment the Bajang had offered them, the team had decided on continuing their delve.

Perhaps they might even break through the third biome this day.

***

The group turned another corner, only to find a group of Adventurers standing in the hallway. Not that that was a surprise, but the exact members were. After all, between Lady Nyssa's Orb and Asin's heightened senses, they had a good idea of what they were walking into on the regular. It was only the high likelihood of being attacked that kept Asin close to the group.

"What are you doing here?" Daniel said, tensing.

Omrak and Zef both spread out in the narrow corridor, the pair of front-line tanks looking worriedly at the five Adventurers before them. The four scruffy Adventurers were less of a concern considering the general lack of repair for their equipment, but the man standing in the front was worrying.

Very worrying.

"Making sure people understand that when I say something, I mean it," Mattias said. He pulled his sword from his scabbard, an action that was mimicked by the others.

"Are you insane?" Lady Nyssa said, calling out. "If you attack us here, our Guild and my family will know who did it. There is no way for you to get away with this."

Mattias smirked. "That's what you think. But right now, *I'm* seated in the Adventurers Guild, having a drink where everyone can see me."

"How?" Daniel asked, curiously.

"A skill, of course. Not that it matters to you," Mattias said. He grinned suddenly, his eyes growing vicious and cold. "Maybe I'll just take you back with me after I cut off your limbs. Then you'll learn to mind your manners properly."

Daniel wanted to point out how dumb it was to threaten a healer, but then again, perhaps Mattias did not care. After all, he could have Daniel heal others and never make use of his services. Punishing Daniel—breaking him—would just be a matter of time then.

"I will not let you harm the lady." The bodyguard spoke up, stepping in front of Lady Nyssa. "But if you allow us to step aside, we will take a vow to keep silent about what might occur here."

"What?" Asin growled, turning from where she stood, her knives appearing in her hand.

"My apologies. My job is to safeguard my charge. I wish you all well," the bodyguard said firmly.

Mattias, on the other hand, was laughing, slapping his thigh and pointing out the bodyguard's betrayal to his men.

"Charles . . ." Lady Nyssa spoke up, her voice surprised and a little tentative.

"Remember, my lady, you have responsibilities above these . . ." Charles swept his gaze over the group dismissively. Turning his head, he called out. "What do you say, Adventurer Mattias? Do we have your word?"

"You have it. But you'll stand to the side till we're done." Mattias leered. "I want your lady to watch."

"Very well." Charles grabbed hold of Lady Nyssa's arm and pulled the reluctant Mage backwards.

Daniel watched them leave, his face twisting with the betrayal before he shook his head. Asin let out a little yowl, her tail jerking from side to side before she turned back to Mattias as he called out.

"Anyone else?" Mattias said. "I want the healer and his original friends. The rest of you can make a vow later . . ."

Daniel turned his head, watching the others. Only to see Zef shake his head in answer. As for Anne, she drew and fired an arrow directly at Mattias. Rather than hit him with the sudden surprise attack, the older Adventurer just smacked it aside contemptuously as he activated **Flawless Parry**.

As though everyone else had been waiting for a sign, both sides surged forwards immediately.

Chapter 14

Anne and Asin were the first to attack. Asin's knives split apart as her skill took the weapon and threw out a **Fan of Knives**, forcing one of the charging Adventurers to throw himself aside and behind a shield-wielding compatriot. Even then, one weapon caught against his calf, scoring it.

Anne's second arrow of the fight on the other hand was a fast-reloaded weapon using her skill **Second Shot**, allowing her to nock and fire again in the blink of an eye. Rather than attack the powerful Mattias, she sent the attack at a halberd-wielding opponent, only for the attack to skitter off at the last moment as a defensive charge overlaid the man's body. Immediately, she began to draw another arrow and moved to find a new angle to fire from as the group clashed.

Zef's greater reach with his weapon let him attack first, though the halberd-wielder he targeted had much the same distance advantage.

The pair thrust and blocked with their polearms, attempting to drive one another back and open a hole for the shorter ranged members of their party.

In the meantime, Omrak threw himself at the pair of other melee attackers who were just getting their footing after dealing with Asin's knives. However, as he was swinging his giant sword, the last attacker fired his own crossbow bolt, the attack plunging into Omrak's shoulder. He groaned, staggering backwards from the pain.

In the meantime, Mattias had held back while Daniel, seeing the danger that Omrak was in as he staggered backwards from the crossbow bolt, rushed forwards. As if that was the signal the experienced Adventurer had been waiting for, he blurred towards Daniel. **Flash Steps** took the Adventurer right up to the healer, and only a reactive block stopped Daniel from being skewered. Even so, his momentum was arrested as Mattias began to strike at him through his shield.

For the next few moments, Daniel was on the backfoot. The attacks rained down on him at such speed that he had no time nor space to attack back, each strike making his shoulder ache. It was obvious that Mattias was both stronger and faster than he was, but beyond his initial use of a skill, he had chosen to focus just on basic attacks. All Daniel could do was keep his attention, allowing the man to hammer on his shield and watch it slowly chip away.

In moments, Daniel was pushed back past the front of the broken melee line. Asin, attempting to help Daniel, had been kicked away contemptuously, sent skittering towards where Omrak had been fending off his attackers. The big Northerner had pulled the crossbow bolt out of his arm, each movement pumping blood as he swung his weapon, though the red haze of **Rage** built up around him. Only Anne's desperate scurry over to him and her healing kept him up.

To Daniel's surprise, instead of two fighters, there were three melee attackers piled on Omrak, the weakest link at the moment. A glimpse under his shield as he was forced to his knees allowed Daniel to spot the remains of a crossbow bolt, its body shattered, the remnants of another arrow by its side. Obviously Anne had dealt with the ranged weapon before she went to help Omrak.

The trio of Adventurers were forced into close proximity against three other melee fighters, while Zef was slowly winning his own solo fight. However, while he might have been more skilled, his opponent was sufficiently versed in the weapon to keep him from helping the others.

As Daniel swung at an ankle with his hammer, he hissed as a sword stabbed into his arm. His hand opened reflexively, the hammer dropping from his arm to bounce off the floor and be dragged back as he yanked his injured limb away. The hammer, held to him by a strap, bounced on his knee as he scrambled away, barely dodging a strike that nearly took his ear but left a line of blood across his cheek.

"You're good at running. But that can't last . . ." Mattias mocked, pushing Daniel back.

The Adventurer groaned, forcing his Gift to patch his arm up enough that he could grip his hammer again.

Out of the corner of Daniel's eyes, he caught sight of Lady Nyssa arguing with the bodyguard who stood by, impassively. Charles's face was impassively calm, content to watch the on-going fight and massacre as long as his charge was safe.

Another cry, and Anne staggered out of the line. The archer and healer clutched at her stomach, attempting to cast a spell to heal herself even as Omrak began taking big swings with his weapon to cover her retreat. That opened him up to further attacks, allowing a couple of quick strikes to score his body.

Daniel's breath heaved, the stink of blood and the sour smell of fear clogging his nostril with each breath. His heart thundered in his chest even as his arm ached from the multiple attacks it had blocked. Another blow, and his poor battered shield gave way. It shattered around his arm, sending Daniel sprawling backwards. Contemptuously, Mattias cut forward, his attack bouncing off the plate mail breastplate that Daniel wore but surprisingly, cutting through it.

On his back now, Daniel was close to the ground. He swung his hand forward, but at the last moment shortened his swing to keep it tight towards his body. Tricked, Mattias's sword briefly dipped, giving Daniel a moment to trigger the enchantment in his axe as he smashed it into the floor.

A swirling light exploded from the hammer and, wary, Mattias jumped backwards. A short moment later, the Swift Ape Alpha he had stored away came into being.

"Kill him!" Daniel cried out, before he sent his own senses back into his injured shield arm.

A flare of power from his Gift and the slipping of a memory set it to healing, before he turned to watch his friends.

For a moment, he debated aiding his beleaguered friends, both Asin and Omrak bleeding from multiple wounds, or joining the attack against Mattias. The Catkin was the worst off, not used to standing and fighting as she was forced to while Omrak's body glowed with red.

Then, just as he was deciding, Omrak roared and threw himself forward. He let a sword skitter off his body as he released the **Lightning's Call**, only to have the entire attack flash forwards to the shield-wielder as they triggered their own skill. **Trouble's Lodestone** ensured that every bolt of lightning struck the enemy's shield, overloading it and the wielder behind with the electricity.

Still, the momentary taunt was enough as the former crossbow-wielder darted outwards, stabbing a blade deep into Omrak's thigh.

Mind made up, Daniel cast his spell, pouring energy into the **Healer's Mark** spell that wrapped around Omrak. He cast a second one on Asin too, hoping that Anne, who darted in to help, could keep the pair fighting.

Because his brief reprieve was over. Mattias had dispatched the powerful Swift Ape with contemptuous ease and was stalking forwards, his blade dripping with blood.

"What a fun little trick . . ." Mattias taunted. "Come, show me another . . ."

He smirked, swinging his sword lazily at Daniel. The Adventurer parried the attack with his own hammer, pulling the weapon down, sparks flashing between the two weapons as they met. But as usual, Mattias ignored the lightning shocks.

Sword pushed out of the way, Mattias stepped in, letting Daniel's left hook strike his body as he smashed an elbow into Daniel's face. His nose crumpled, blood spurting from the injury as he staggered back, only for Mattias to kick him again in the chest and send him skipping back, even further from his friend.

As he struggled up, Mattias laughed.

"I told you, you should have joined us."

Another attack, the blade plunging into Daniel's shoulder. He screamed as Mattias twisted the blade, disabling his weapon arm. Mattias smirked, raising his weapon as he grabbed hold of Daniel's other arm, his weapon raised.

"Now, let's see how you do without your arm. You can use your nose to heal people, right? It's just touch . . ."

***

The sword swung down, and Daniel screamed as he futilely tried to get away. Yet it never finished its progress down, the sword flicking to the side suddenly as Daniel and Mattias both spun away. An arrow shattered, its iron head broken apart, as Mattias once more triggered **Flawless Parry** and blocked the attack from Charles.

"Did you think I would not expect betrayal?" Mattias said gloatingly.

In answer, Lady Nyssa finally finished her spell and thrust her hands forwards. The **Cone of Noise**, a high screeching attack that struck Mattias directly in the face made him grunt and twist. His nose and ears burst with blood as Daniel felt his own teeth and hearing ache from the proximity.

Yet he did not fall, nor did he let go of Daniel's arm. Instead, he threw his sword underhand at the Mage. Charles in turn moved his body to block the attack, the blade plunging into his body and forcing him to his knees while Lady Nyssa had to cut off her attack or hit her own man.

"Idiot children," Mattias said as he reached for the sheathed knife on his side.

Eyes wide, Lady Nyssa scrambled to get another spell off. Daniel felt a pit of dread open in his stomach, understanding flooding into his mind. There was no way that Lady Nyssa could get a spell off before he cut her down. In fact, it was clear that Mattias was just playing with them. And the moment he was done, his joining the desperate fight between the other Adventurers would spell the end of them.

Once again, Daniel cast around for something, anything he could do. He pulled at his arm, barely even jostling the grip. Mattias didn't bother to look at Daniel as he struggled, so dismissive was Mattias of anything Daniel could do. And why shouldn't he be? Without a weapon, Daniel had no skills to use. He had no attack spells. And his Gift . . .

His Gift.

Eyes widening a little, Daniel plunged into his own body and mind. He reached for his Gift, acting before he could think further about what he was choosing to do. He entered Mattias's body, flooding into it and felt the other man tense a little. He probably could only barely sense what Daniel was doing, but instinct had him looking down, reacting.

Too slow. For Daniel was acting at the speed of thought and will.

A touch here. A small push there. A tap turned off.

And Mattias collapsed, bonelessly, nerves in the base of his spine no longer sending signals.

Now, it was Daniel gripping an unresponsive arm as he made a few additional minor alterations. Blood vessels leading from the heart were torn open. He let the chest cavity fill, as the heart struggled to pump blood out, only to spill it inwards again.

Mattias, eyes wide, could only stare at Daniel as his body flooded from within, and his body began to fail. Daniel struggled up to his feet, only for Charles to stagger over, a short sword held in one hand, ready to stab the man.

"Don't bother," Daniel said, his voice tightly controlled. Controlled, because at the edges of his mind, the horror at what he had done attempted to escape. He had killed with his Gift, and Daniel could only wonder if Erlis herself would strike him down for taking her healing Gift and making it a weapon.

Charles stared at the unmoving body and the darting eyes of their tormentor that were clouding over in death before he nodded at Daniel. Turning, the bodyguard lumbered forwards to join the other fight, only to be beaten to it by Lady Nyssa.

A screaming orb flew past his head, flying towards the group and past them to explode in a large, painful attack at the back of the opposing Adventurers. The entire group staggered, but at least Daniel and team were somewhat ready, the frontline fighters provided minor talismans to help ward off such damage. Even as the group before them staggered, ears aching, the Seven Stones team reacted.

Omrak stabbed outwards with his large sword, impaling an unsuspecting Adventurer under the arm, piercing the chainmail covering meant to protect such attacks. Pushing forwards, Omrak twisted his weapon at the same time before he extracted it, leaving his opponent with a large gushing wound as he collapsed from the pain.

At the same time, Asin jumped forward, low to the ground. She slid between a pair of legs and under the raised shield that the opposition used as he clutched at his head. As she twisted around, her blades flashed as she triggered **Penetration**, the weapons tearing into her opponent's hamstrings. As he fell forwards, Asin tucked her feet up to her body and then kicked outwards, sending her opponent flying forwards onto his face and towards Anne, who stabbed down at the exposed neck.

Their last opponent had turned to run, having seen where things were going. Yet he failed to make it more than a few steps before a spear caught him in the thigh, piercing his body as Zef triggered **Unerring Strike**, pushing the spearhead into the man's back. As the

Adventurer stumbled and fell, Zef kept the pressure up, striking him again and again.

And just like that, the fight was over.

Daniel staggered to his feet, already having cast a **Healer's Mark** on himself. A part of him was doing triage, trying to work out how many casts he had left and who needed immediate healing, who could last with a **Healer's Mark** and who required a potion immediately.

There was much that he needed to do, to say.

Now, if only he could find a way to get rid of the horror deep within his soul at what he had done.

Chapter 15

"Publicly, they'll disavow his actions," Gadi was saying, his words droning on to explain how the Three Skills were going to handle the matter. It all amounted to a lot of nothing that could be done to them—publicly at least. Gadi hinted at other restrictions placed on them, but to Daniel, the words just continued on like the buzzing of a really annoying insect. The rest of the team paid much more attention, listening to Gadi as they sat around the board room table within the guild's building.

After the fight and healing, the team had dragged the bodies back up to the Dungeon entrance. Their appearance, with multiple bodies in tow, had caused quite a bit of a disturbance, enough that the Adventurers Hall had immediately sent administrators and guards to begin an investigation. The entire group had to subject themselves to multiple interrogations with truth stones in play. Gadi had watched over all such interrogations before they were eventually released to return to the Seven Stones compound.

A full day of investigation had continued. Daniel had fallen asleep the moment they had been returned, his body and mind exhausted from the travails. Now, he sat listening, or trying to. Yet his mind felt like it was fogged over, thoughts and words finding themselves lost the instant they entered his ears, an impenetrable fog keeping him floating.

It was how he found himself standing on a balcony, staring down at the training grounds, one hand clutched around the stone bannister. His mind buzzed with the spell of healing that Anne, down below, was casting. A part of him wanted to shout at her, at how dangerous that was.

A part of him wanted to help and correct her.

And a part of him just watched, uncaring.

A hand fell upon Daniel's shoulder, fingers big, palms wide, and the entire thing heavy. Daniel turned, blinking to see Guildmaster

Parndo, who had been at the meeting earlier, but other than reassuring and apologizing to them all had been silent as Gadi did the talking.

"What ails you, healer?" Parndo said.

"Don't call me that," Daniel said, automatically.

"What? Healer? That is what you are, is it not?" Parndo frowned. "Or did I mistake you for another? I'm pretty sure I remembered you right."

"No. I was a healer. I'm not now . . ." Daniel's voice hitched a bit at the end.

"Tell me." The words were a command rather than a gentle request.

But Daniel found himself wanting to speak anyway, his words spilling out in a rush. When he finally wound down, when he found himself trying to explain his dread and how he was no healer, Parndo held a hand up.

Daniel clamped his mouth shut, and the guildmaster nodded. "I see no problem with what you did. You killed an Adventurer more skilled than you, using your Gift. Good."

"It was meant for healing!" Daniel shouted, shuddering. He did not speak about what he had lost, what memories had fled. He was not sure, not really. But a part of him wondered if it was more or less than what he usually lost. He had only tapped in for a few seconds, but he had done something anathema to the Gift.

"Are you sure?" Parndo said. "Way I understand Gifts, we don't exactly get a manual with it. Could be that you've been using it wrong all this time."

"It literally is called **Martyr's Touch** and speaks about healing!" Daniel said, heatedly.

"Right, right. But I knew a guy who could create barriers to protect. Used to make them form inside bodies. Really effective at killing," Parndo said. "Anyway, it doesn't matter. I agree, you aren't much of a healer." Daniel blinked, surprised at being agreed with. "Way I see it, you're more of an Adventurer than anything else. That's what you decided, isn't it?"

"I . . ."

"Otherwise, you wouldn't be here. You'd be swanning around the capital as the royals' healer or maybe hiding away in some small village, patching up sore feet." Parndo waved a hand down to the training grounds. "Way I see it, you're just like the rest of us. Adventurers."

"That's . . . I . . ."

Parndo ignored Daniel, continuing to speak. "And Adventurers, we just do what it takes to get the job done." A pause, then he turned to stare at Daniel. "Even if it is breaking a few rules."

Daniel clamped his mouth shut, a mulish expression growing on his face.

"Anyway, that's the way I see it. Then again, I'm not much of a thinker. Much better at just hitting things." Grinning, Parndo clapped Daniel on the shoulder. "Either way, you should be training. We'll let you know once we get the bodies back and what equipment there was. Probably nothing great, but you never know. And don't you worry, we'll handle the Three Skills. They won't bother you no more."

After finishing, Parndo pushed Daniel into the hallway before turning back to staring out at the other Adventurers. Daniel glared at the guildmaster's back for a moment before he sighed and trundled off.

He could not help but shake his head a little as he walked away, muttering to himself as he did so. "Not much of a pep talk."

But, strangely enough, he did find himself a little happier.

Just a little, mind you.

Epilogue

Two weeks later, Daniel was crouched beside his friend, staring around the corner of the passageway leading into the deep cavern before them. Around him, his party crouched as Daniel took in the Floor Boss that slept right next to the staircase to the seventh floor. The Bajang Alpha Floor Boss was thrice the size of the largest Bajang they had seen, a monstrous creature that was at least eleven feet long—not including its tail that sparked with lightning—and whose body shimmered, fading in and out of the shadows even as it lay at rest.

His party. Daniel could not help but glance at them all, his eyes stopping on Lady Nyssa and Charles, her bodyguard. Their betrayal—faked perhaps or real, he was still not certain truly—had been what had turned the tables. That they had made plans without the rest of them was disturbing to Daniel, yet it had been successful. And so they had stayed.

Even if everyone else gave them the side-eye once in a while.

Not that those had been the only scars left by the attack. Sure, they had received a hefty payout and even a few enchanted pieces of equipment. The attacking group had been quite rich, all things considered, though they had taken ill care of their equipment. Still, distributed through the group, it had left most with an additional enchanted equipment.

Mattias's equipment had been the most bountiful, though none of the party actually wielded a sword—the most expensive and enchanted piece that Mattias had owned. That had been exchanged with the guild to allow the group to pick up three other lesser-powered pieces.

All in all, the party had come out of the situation better equipped and richer. Yet they were jumpier, less prone to taking risks, and more paranoid about meeting others. It had slowed their initial delves, especially since Daniel had not joined them at first.

The few weeks after the fight had passed to a blur for Daniel, he still wasn't reconciled with what he had done. More nights than not, he woke up screaming from a nightmare that he could not remember. Yet, he had finally found himself down here with his friends, forced to come down because, in the end, this was what he wanted. What he had dreamed of.

Fighting monsters. Cleansing Dungeons. Being an Adventurer.

And knowing that, there was only one thing he could do.

Keep delving.

The End

Daniel continues his life as an Adventurer in book 8 of the Adventurers on Brad –

A Capital's Perils

Author's Note

If you enjoyed reading the book, please leave a review and rating. Not only is it a big ego boost, it also helps sales and convinces me to write more in the series! Continue following Daniel's adventures in the next book:

- A Capital's Perils (Book 8 of the Adventures in Brad series)
  https://books2read.com/capitals-perils

In addition, please check out my other series. I have written the System Apocalypse (a post-apocalyptic LitRPG), A Thousand Li (a xianxia cultivation story) and the Hidden Wishes (an urban fantasy GameLit). Book one of each series follow:

- Life in the North (Book 1 of the System Apocalypse)
  https://books2read.com/life-in-the-north

- A Gamer's Wish (Book 1 of the Hidden Wishes series)
  https://books2read.com/gamers-wish

- A Thousand Li: the First Step (Book 1 of the A Thousand Li series) https://books2read.com/atl-first-step

For more great information about great LitRPG series, check out the Facebook groups:

- GameLit Society: https://www.facebook.com/groups/LitRPGsociety/
- LitRPG Books: https://www.facebook.com/groups/LitRPG.books/

About the Author

Tao Wong is an avid fantasy and sci-fi reader who spends his time working and writing in the North of Canada. He's spent way too many years doing martial arts of many forms and having broken himself too often, now spends his time writing about fantasy worlds.

If you'd like to support him directly, Tao now has a Patreon page where previews of all his new books can be found!

- https://www.patreon.com/taowong

For updates on the series and his other books (and special one-shot stories), please visit the author's website:
https://www.mylifemytao.com

Subscribers to Tao's mailing list will receive exclusive access to short stories in the Thousand Li and System Apocalypse universes:
https://www.subscribepage.com/taowong

Or visit Tao's Facebook Page:
https://www.facebook.com/taowongauthor/

About the Publisher

Starlit Publishing is wholly owned and operated by Tao Wong. It is a science fiction and fantasy publisher focused on the LitRPG & cultivation genres. Their focus is on promoting new, upcoming authors in the genre whose writing challenges the existing stereotypes while giving a rip-roaring good read.

For more information on Starlit Publishing, visit their website:
https://www.starlitpublishing.com/

You can also join Starlit Publishing's mailing list to learn of new, exciting authors and book releases:
https://starlitpublishing.com/newsletter-signup/

Books in the Adventures on Brad series

A Healer's Gift

An Adventurer's Heart

A Dungeon's Soul

The Arena's Call

The Adventurers Bond

The Forest's Silence

The Guild's Demands

A Capital's Perils

A Royal Ending